KU-061-761

Point Horror

THE FORBIDDEN GAME

3: THE KILL

L.J. Smith

SCHOLASTIC

Scholastic Children's Books,
7-9 Pratt Street, London NW1 0AE, UK
a division of Scholastic Ltd
London ~ New York ~ Toronto ~ Sydney ~ Auckland

First published in the US by Simon & Schuster Inc., 1994
First published in the UK by Scholastic Ltd, 1995

Copyright © Lisa J. Smith, 1994

ISBN 0 590 13244 X

Printed by Cox and Wyman Ltd, Reading, Berks

10 9 8 7 6 5 4 3 2 1

All rights reserved

The right of Lisa J. Smith to be identified as the author of this work has been asserted by her in accordance with the Copyright, Designs and Patents Act, 1988.

This book is sold subject to the condition that it shall not, by way of trade or otherwise be lent, resold, hired out, or otherwise circulated without the publisher's prior consent in any form of binding or cover other than that in which it is published and without a similar condition, including this condition, being imposed upon the subsequent purchaser.

THE FORBIDDEN GAME

3: THE KILL

Then the whispering began. It started so softly that at first she thought it might be the blood rushing in her ears. But it was real. The voices were distant and musical – and menacing. What they were saying was too indistinct to be made out.

Shoulders hunched, Jenny turned her head slowly, trying to locate the sound. And there, in the darkness, she saw eyes.

They glowed with their own light, like firefox. They were cold, ravenous. She recognized them from her grandfather's closet.

The Shadow Men.

Look out for:

Fatal Secrets
Richie Tankersley Cusick

Driver's Dead
Peter Lerangis

The Boy Next Door
Sinclair Smith

For the *real* Sue Carson, the inspiration for her namesake. And for John G. Check III, with love and thanks.

1

The flight attendant started toward them, and the back of Jenny's neck began to prickle. Her little fingers tingled.

Be casual, she told herself. Be calm.

But her heart began to pound as the flight attendant reached their row. She was dressed in navy blue with cream accents and looked rather military. Her face was pleasant but authoritative, like an alert teacher.

Don't look at her. Look out the window.

Jenny wedged her fingernails into the bottom of the plastic trim around the oval window and stared at the darkness outside. She could feel Michael beside her, his teddy-bear-shaped body rigid with tension. Out of the corner of her eye she could see Audrey in the aisle seat, her burnished copper head bent over the in-flight magazine. The flight attendant was blocking the view of Dee across the aisle.

Please let her go away, Jenny thought. Please, anything, why is she *standing* there so long?

Any minute now Michael was going to break into hysterical giggles—or, worse, a hysterical confession. Without moving a muscle, Jenny silently willed him to stay quiet. The flight attendant *had* to go away. She couldn't just keep standing there.

She did. It became clear that she wasn't just stopping casually, a little rest on the route from the galley. She was *looking* at them, looking at each of them in turn. A grave, searching look.

We're debate club students, flying to the finals. Our chaperon got sick, but we're meeting a new one in Pittsburgh. We're debate club students, flying to the finals. Our chaperon got sick, but . . .

The flight attendant leaned toward Jenny.

Oh, my God, I'm going to be sick.

Audrey stayed frozen over her magazine, spiky lashes motionless on her camellia-pale cheek. Michael stopped breathing.

Calm, calm, calm, calm . . .

"Is it you," the flight attendant said, "who ordered the fruit plate?"

Jenny's mind swooped into a nosedive and stalled. For a terrible second she thought she was going to go ahead and babble out the excuse she'd been practicing. Then she licked the dry roof of her mouth and whispered, "No. It's her—across the aisle there."

The flight attendant backed up and turned. Dee, with one long leg folded so she could tuck her toe into the little pouch on the back of the seat in front of her, lifted her eyes from her Gameboy and smiled.

Except for the Gameboy and the army fatigue jacket she was wearing, she looked exactly like Nefertiti. Even her smile was regal.

"Fruit plate," the flight attendant said. "Seat eighteen-D. Lovely, got it." The next moment she was gone.

"You and your damned, damned fruit plates," Jenny hissed across the aisle. And to Michael: "For God's sake, Michael, breathe!"

Michael let out his breath with a *whoosh.*

"What could they do to us, anyway?" Audrey said. She was still looking at her magazine, and she spoke without moving her lips, her voice barely audible above the deep roar of the 757's engines. "Throw us off? We're six miles up."

"Don't remind me," Jenny said to the window as Michael began to describe to Audrey, in hushed detail, exactly what he imagined they could do with four runaways in Pittsburgh.

Runaways. I'm a runaway, Jenny thought wonderingly. It was such an unlikely thing for her, Jenny Thornton, to be.

In the darkened window she could see her own face—or part of it. A girl with forest-green eyes, dark as pine needles, and eyebrows that were straight, like two decisive brush strokes. Hair the color of honey in sunlight.

Jenny looked past the ghostly reflection to the black clouds outside the plane. Now that the stewardess danger had passed, all she had to worry about was dying.

She *really* hated heights.

What was strange was that even though she was scared, she was also excited. The way people get excited when an emergency, a natural disaster, happens. When all normal rules are suspended, and ordinary things that used to be important suddenly become meaningless.

Like school. Like her parents' approval. Like being a good girl.

All blown when she ran away. And her parents wouldn't even understand why, because the note Jenny had left them had said almost nothing. *I'm going somewhere and I hope I'll come back. I love you. This is something I have to do.*

I'm sorry. IOU $600.00.

Not very informative. But what was she supposed to say? *Dear Mom and Dad, A terrible thing happened at Tom's birthday party last month. You see, we built this paper house and it became real. And suddenly we were all inside it, and this guy called Julian made us play a game there with him. We had to face our worst nightmares and win, or he would have kept us with him in the Shadow World forever. And we all made it out except Summer—poor Summer, you know she was never the brightest—and that's why Summer's been missing for weeks. She died in her nightmare.*

But the thing is, Mom and Dad, that Julian followed *us out of the Shadow World. He came into our world and he was after one thing—me.* Me. *He made us play another game, and this one turned out bad. It ended with him taking Tom and Zach back to the Shadow World. That's where they are now—they didn't run away like everybody thinks. And the last thing Julian said to me after taking them was: If you want them, come on a treasure hunt.*

So that's what I'm doing. Only there's just a slight problem about getting into the Shadow World—I don't have any idea how to do it. So I'm flying to Pennsylvania, to Grandpa Evenson's house. He opened a door to the Shadow World a long time ago, and maybe he left some clues behind.

Say that? God, no, Jenny thought. The first part her parents had already heard, and didn't believe. The second part would just let them know where Jenny was going—and give them a chance to stop her. *Excuse me, Doctor, but my daughter has flipped. She thinks some demon prince has taken her boyfriend and her cousin. We've got to lock her up and keep her safe. Oh, yes, get that* biiiiig *hypodermic over there.*

No, Jenny couldn't tell anyone. She and Audrey and Dee and Michael had spent three days planning this trip. It had taken them that long to get enough money for plane tickets, each collecting two hundred dollars a day using their parents' ATM cards. Now they were on the red-eye from LAX to Pittsburgh, alone and vulnerable, six miles off the ground. Their parents thought they were asleep in their beds.

And Jenny was excited. Do or die. It was do or die, now, literally. There wasn't such a thing as safety anymore. She was going to a place where nightmares came true—and killed you. She would never forget Summer's blond head disappearing in that pile of garbage.

When she got there, all she'd have to rely on were her own wits—and her friends.

She glanced at them. Michael Cohen, with his rumpled dark hair and soulful eyes, wearing clothes that were clean, wrinkled, and bore no resemblance to any fashion trend that had ever existed. Audrey Myers, cool and elegant in a black-and-white Italian pantsuit, keeping any turmoil she might be feeling hidden under a perfectly polished exterior. And Dee Eliade, a night princess with a skewed sense of humor and a black belt in kung fu. They were all sixteen, juniors in high school, and they were on their way to fight the devil.

The flight attendants served dinner. Dee ate her fruit plate brazenly. Once the trays were cleared, lights began to go out all over the plane. One by one they winked off.

Funeral parlor lighting, Jenny thought, looking at the dim, diffused ceiling-glow that was left. It reminded her of the visitation room where she'd last seen her great-aunt Sheila. She felt too keyed-up to sleep, but she had to try.

Think of anything but *him,* she ordered herself, leaning her head against the cool, vibrating wall of the plane. Oh, who cares, think of him if you want to. He's lost his power over you. The part of you that rushed up to meet his darkness is gone. This time you can beat him—because you don't feel anything for him.

To prove it, she let images drift through her mind. Julian laughing at her, his face beautiful in the most exotic, uncanny way imaginable—more beautiful than any human's could ever be. Julian's hair, as white as frost, as tendrils of mist. No, whiter than that, an impossible icy color. His eyes just as impossible. A blue that she couldn't describe because there was nothing to compare it to.

As long as she was proving a point, she could remember other things, too. His body, slim but powerfully built, hard-muscled when he held her close. His touch all the more shockingly soft. His long, slow kisses—so slow, so confident, because he was absolutely certain of what he was doing. He might look like a boy Jenny's age, he might be the youngest of his kind, but he was older than Jenny could imagine. He was expert far beyond her experience. He'd had girls through the centuries, any he wanted, all helpless to resist his touch in the darkness.

Jenny's lips parted, her tongue against her teeth. Maybe this wasn't such a good idea after all. Julian had no power over her, but it was stupid to tempt fate by thinking about him.

She would think of Tom instead, of little Tommy kissing her behind the ficus bushes in second grade, of Tom Locke, star of the athletic field. Of his hazel eyes with their flecks of green, his neat dark hair, his devil-may-care smile. Of the way he looked at her when he whispered, "Oh, Thorny, I love you"—as if the words themselves hurt him.

He was only human—not some eerily beautiful prince of shadows. He was real, and human, and her equal . . . and he needed her. Especially now.

Jenny wasn't going to betray his trust. She was going to find him and bring him back from the hellish place Julian had taken him. And once she got him safe, she wasn't going to let him go again.

She relaxed. Just the thought of Tom brought her

comfort. In a few minutes her thoughts unwound, and then . . .

She was in an elevator. A silver mask covered the little man's entire face. He was so small she wondered if he was a dwarf.

"Will you go with us? Can we take you?" Jenny realized he'd been asking the same question for quite some time.

"We can carry you," he said. Jenny was frightened.

"No," she said. "Who are you?"

He kept asking it. "Can we take you?" On the elevator wall behind him was a large poster of Joyland Park, an amusement park that Jenny had loved as a kid. "Can we take you?"

Finally she said, "Yes . . ." and he leaned forward eagerly, his eyes flashing in the mask's eyeholes.

"We can?"

"Yes . . . if you tell me who you really are," she said.

The little man fell back, disappointed.

"Tell me who you really are," Jenny demanded. She was holding a bottle over his head, ready to brain him. She knew somehow that he wasn't actually there; it was only his image. But she thought he might materialize briefly to show her what he really was.

He didn't. Jenny kept hitting the image, but the bottle just swung through it. Then the image disappeared.

Jenny was pleased. She'd proved he wasn't real and that she was in control.

The elevator stopped. Jenny walked through the open doors—into another elevator.

"Can we take you? We can carry you."

The little man in the silver mask was laughing.

Jenny's head jerked up and she sat staring. A plane. She was in a plane, not an elevator. A plane which, at the moment, seemed crammed to its dim corners with menace. She was alone, because everyone else was asleep. The other passengers could all have been wax museum figures. Beside her Michael was completely motionless, his head on Audrey's shoulder.

As she watched, his eyes flew open and he made a terrible sound. He sat bolt upright, hands at his throat. He looked like someone who couldn't get air.

"What is it?" Audrey had jerked awake. There were times when Audrey acted as if she didn't care about Michael at all, but this wasn't one of them.

Michael went on staring, looking absolutely terrified. Jenny's skin was rippling with fear.

"Michael, can you breathe? Are you all right?" Audrey said.

He did breathe, then, a long shaky intake of air. He let it out and slumped back against the seat. His dark brown eyes, normally heavy-lidded, were still wide.

"I had a dream."

"You, too?" Jenny said. Dee was leaning over the armrest of her seat across the aisle. Other people were looking at them, disturbed from sleep. Jenny avoided their eyes.

"What about?" she said, keeping her voice low. "Was it—it wasn't about an elevator, was it?" She had no idea what her own dream meant, but she felt sure it was bad.

"What? No. It was about Summer," he said, licking his lips as if to get rid of a bad taste.

"Oh . . ."

"But it wasn't all of Summer. It was her head. It was on a table, and it was talking to me."

A sensation of unspeakable horror washed over Jenny.

That was when the plane plummeted.

2

Jenny screamed. It didn't matter, everyone was screaming. Dee, who had unbuckled her seat belt to lean toward Michael, was bounced upward so hard her head almost hit the ceiling.

They were falling, and the sensation was worse than a thousand elevators. There was nothing beneath Jenny because the seat was falling away.

What do people think about when they're going to die? What should I be thinking?

Tom. She should think about Tom and how she loved him. But it was impossible, there was no room inside her for anything but astonishment and fear.

Then the plane lurched up. Instead of falling, her seat was pressing against her. The whole thing had taken only a second or so.

The pilot's voice came on over the intercom, smooth and rich as cream soda. "Ah, sorry about that, folks—we hit a little turbulence. We're going to try to get above this weather; in the meantime please keep your seat belts fastened."

Just turbulence. Ordinary stuff. They weren't going to die.

Jenny looked out the window again. She couldn't see much; they were in the middle of clouds. Mist and darkness—

Just like the mist and darkness the Shadow Men bring, her mind raced on irresistibly. Any minute now you'll see the eyes, the hungry, hungry eyes . . .

But she didn't see anything.

"Hey, listen," Michael was saying huskily. "About my dream—"

"It was just a dream," Audrey said, ever practical. Jenny was grateful for the little edge in Audrey's voice, the sharp edge of reason. Like a wake-up slap.

"Just a dream. Didn't mean anything," Jenny echoed—unfairly, because she didn't for a moment believe that. But she had no idea what it *did* mean, and ganging up on Michael was the only comfort available. Was Julian behind it? Torturing them with images of Summer? Nightmares were the Shadow Man's specialty.

The Shadow Man. Like the Sandman, only he brings nightmares. And by now he knows us all, knows our weak points. He can bring our worst fears to life, and they may not be real, but we won't be able to tell the difference.

What are we getting into?

She spent the rest of the flight staring out the oval window, her hands clutching the cold metal ends of her armrests.

* * *

Pittsburgh at 6:56 A.M. was cool. Breezy. The sky a blue that early morning skies in southern California seldom aspired to. In Vista Grande, where Jenny lived, May skies were usually the color of wet concrete until it got hot enough to break the clouds up.

They had to take a taxi from the airport because Hertz wouldn't rent a car to anyone under twenty-five. Dee thought this was outrageous and wanted to argue, but Jenny dragged her away.

"We're trying to be inconspicuous," she said.

On the way to Monessen they saw a river with large, flat, ugly ships on it. "The Monongahela and coal barges," Jenny said, remembering. They saw delicate trees with slender trunks and airy little pink buds. "Redbud trees," Jenny said. "And those over there with the white flowers are dogwoods." They saw one steel mill with white smoke turning to gray as it rose. "There used to be blast furnaces all over here," Jenny said. "When they were going, it looked like hell. Really. All these chimneys with fire and black smoke coming out of them. When I was a kid, I thought that was what hell must look like."

By the time they got to the little town of Monessen, Michael was eyeing the taxi meter with deep concern. Everyone else, though, was staring out the windows.

"Cobblestone streets," Dee said. "D'you believe that?"

"C'est drôle ca," Audrey said. "How quaint."

"They're not *all* cobblestone," Jenny said.

"They're all steep," Dee said.

Because the town was built on hills—seven hills,

Jenny remembered. When she and Zach had been kids here, that had seemed a magical fact, like a seventh son of a seventh son being psychic.

Don't think about Zach now. And especially don't think about Tom. But, as always, Tom's name alone started an aching in her chest. Like a bruise just slightly to the left of her breastbone.

"We're here," she said aloud, forcibly distracting herself.

"Three Center Drive," the taxi driver said and got out to unload their duffel bags from the trunk.

Audrey, whose father was with the diplomatic corps and who had grown up all over the world, paid the man. She knew how to do things like that, and carried it off with cosmopolitan flair, adding an extravagant tip.

"Money—" Michael began in an anguished whisper. Audrey ignored him. The taxi drove off.

Jenny held her breath as she looked around. All the way from Pittsburgh she'd had flashes of familiarity. But here, in front of her grandfather's house, the familiarity came in a great, sweeping rush, engulfing her.

I know this! I know this place! I remember!

Of course she remembered. She'd grown up here. The broad green lawn that grew all the way to the street with no sidewalk in between—she and Zach had played there. This low brick house with the little white porch—she couldn't tell how many times she'd gone running up to it.

It was a strange sort of remembering, though. The house seemed smaller, and not exactly the way she'd pictured it. Old and new at the same time.

Maybe because it's been empty for ten years, Jenny thought. Or maybe it's changed—

No. It hadn't changed—*she* had. The last time she'd stood here she'd been five years old.

And the memory of *that* was like a light splash of icy water. It reminded her of what she'd come here to do.

Am I brave enough? Am I really brave enough to go back down to that room and face everything that happened there?

A slender arm, hard as a boy's, went around her shoulders. Jenny blinked back wetness and saw that everyone was looking at her. Audrey was standing silently, her glossy auburn hair shining like copper in the early morning light. Her chestnut eyes were quietly sympathetic. Michael's round face was solemn.

Dee, with her arm still around Jenny, gave a barbaric grin.

"C'mon, Tiger. Let's do it," she said.

Jenny let out her breath and tried to grin the same way herself. "Around back. There should be, um, stone steps down to the basement and a back door. If memory serves."

Memory did. On the back porch Dee pulled a crowbar out of her duffel bag.

They'd come prepared. In the duffel bags there were also towels to lay over the frames of any windows they might have to break, and a hammer, and a screwdriver.

"It's a good thing the house is empty. If it weren't, we couldn't do this," Dee said, placing the crowbar judiciously.

"If it weren't, there wouldn't be any point in doing it," Jenny said. "Whoever moved in would have cleared out the basement. For that matter, we can't be sure somebody *hasn't—"*

"Wait!" Audrey yelled.

Everyone froze.

"Look at that." Audrey pointed to something beside the door. A black-and-silver sticker with curling edges. When Michael wiped the dirt off with his fingers, Jenny could make out lettering.

THIS PROPERTY PROTECTED BY MONONGAHELA VALLEY SECURITY. ARMED RESPONSE.

"A security alarm," Michael said. "Oh, terrific."

Audrey looked at Jenny. "Do you think it's still working?"

Dee was still holding the crowbar at the door. "We can try and see," she said, grinning.

"No, we can't," Jenny said. "That's just exactly what we can't do. If it *is* working, we won't be able to come back today, because *they'll* be all over the place."

"I think we're in fairly serious trouble here," Michael said.

Jenny shut her eyes.

Why hadn't she thought of this? Her grandfather had probably always had that alarm system—but it wasn't the kind of thing a kid would notice.

But I'm not a kid anymore. I should have thought *now.*

"There's got to be a way to get in," Dee was saying.

"Why?" Audrey's voice was snappish—because she felt bad, Jenny knew. Because she was scared.

"There doesn't always have to be a way just because you want one, Dee."

Think, Jenny. Think, think, think. You forgot the alarm—is there anything else you've forgotten?

"If we're going to get philosophical—" Michael began.

"Mrs. Durash," said Jenny.

They all looked at her.

"She was my grandfather's housekeeper. Maybe she still takes care of the place. Maybe she has a key."

"Brilliant!" Dee said and finally removed the crowbar.

"We've got to find her telephone number—oh, God, if she still even *lives* here. There should be a phone at—at—oh, I guess the dairy bar. It's that way, I think. It's a long walk."

Michael looked cagey. "I'll stay here and guard the bags."

"You'll come with us, and like it," Audrey said. "We can hide the bags in the bushes."

"Yes, dear," Michael muttered. "Yes, dear, yes, dear . . ."

Petro's Dairy Bar, like everything they had passed on the way, had an air of gently going to seed. Jenny stepped into the blue-and-white metal booth outside and was relieved to find a phone book dangling from a chain. She balanced it on her knee and thumbed pages.

"Yes! B. Durash—there *can't* be another Durash in Monessen. It's got to be her."

She stuck in a quarter and dialed before she realized she hadn't planned out what to say.

"Hel-lo." The voice on the other end made the word sound almost like *yellow*. There was a faint accent, earthy, not as slow as a drawl.

"Hi. Hi. Uh, this is Jenny Thornton and—" Debate team, Jenny thought. Vacation, hometown, late spring break—parents. Where are my parents supposed to be?

"Is this Mrs. Durash?" she blurted.

There was a pause that seemed very long. Then: "Mrs. Durash isn't here right now. This is her daughter-in-law."

"Oh . . . but she does live there? Mrs. Durash? And—look, okay, do you happen to know if she's the same Mrs. Durash that worked for Mr. Eric Evenson?" I am making a total fool of myself, Jenny realized, staring at the graffiti on the glass door.

Another pause. "Ye-e-es, she's the caretaker for the Evenson house."

Wonderful! Caretakers *had* to have keys. Jenny was so buoyed up that she forgot about making a fool of herself.

"Thank you—that's great. I mean—it'll be really great to talk to her. Do you know when she'll be back?"

"She always goes over to her son's in Charleroi on Saturday. She'll be back around seven. Call then."

"Seven P.M.?" Michael said bitterly when Jenny repeated the conversation. He flopped onto the splintered green bench against the dairy bar wall. "And we have to wait outside until then. I'm not walking back until I get some ice cream."

"Money," Audrey said with a toss of her copper head.

A bus roared up to the corner. Jenny stared at it absently as she thought. Nine hours to kill. They'd be conspicuous in this little town. They'd have to hide in her grandfather's backyard or—

Something on the side of the bus came into focus. JOYLAND PARK, ROLLER COASTER CAPITAL OF THE WORLD. The poster was illustrated with roller coasters and merry-go-rounds.

The wooden bench seemed to drop away beneath Jenny.

When she could breathe again, the bus was revving its engine to drive away. Jenny made her decision in an instant.

"Let's go!"

Dee bounded up, ready at once. Michael leaned his head against the wall and shut his eyes. Audrey said, "Where?"

"On that bus. Come on, quick!" Jenny ran up and grabbed the dusty glass door before it could straighten shut. "Do you go to Joyland Park?" she shouted.

"Clairton, Duquesne, West Mifflin—West Mifflin's Joyland," he said laconically.

"Right. Four, please."

The others straggled up the steps. The bus was almost empty and smelled like old tires. They sat on the torn leather seats in the very back, and Audrey looked at Jenny.

"Now will you please explain where we're going?"

"Joyland Park," Jenny said a little breathlessly.

"Why?"

"'Cause they've got corn dogs," Michael said, very quietly.

Jenny looked Audrey straight in the eye. "Did you

see that poster on the side of the bus? It was in my dream. I had a dream on the plane, while Michael was dreaming about Summer, and that poster was in it."

Audrey considered, teeth set in her cherry-glossed lower lip. "It might be perfectly natural. You might have had the park on your mind, since you were coming back here and all."

"Or it might be something else," Jenny said. "Like —I don't know, some kind of a message." She shifted. "Look, do any of you ever wonder if—well, if Summer is really dead?"

Audrey looked shocked. Dee said dryly, "We've been telling the police so for a month."

But Michael, eyes round and thoroughly awake now, said, "She was alive in my dream. She talked just like her."

Jenny felt uneasy. "What did she say?"

"She was mad at us for leaving her. She was scared."

Jenny felt even more uneasy. Audrey said, "So you think maybe both dreams were connected or something? And that it was some kind of a message?"

"I don't know. It's so complicated. And I don't even know why anyone could possibly want to send us to an amusement park. . . ." She could feel herself deflating.

"Never mind." Dee grinned wickedly and thumped her on the back. "You went with your instinct; that can't be wrong. And even if it wasn't a message—so what? It's an amusement park. Good, clean fun. Right, guys?"

"I'd rather go shopping," Audrey said. "But it's a way to kill the time."

Michael slumped and jammed his knees against the battered metal seat in front of him. "And kill our money. Did I ever tell you about this amusement park nightmare I had when I was a kid—?"

"Shut up, Michael," three female voices chorused, and he shut up.

It was a long, rather lonely drive to West Mifflin. Joyland Park seemed to be one of the few places still in business in a rundown and isolated area. It was almost a surprise to find it out here, in the middle of nowhere.

Michael made an inarticulate noise of awe as they filed off the bus. "Good grief," he said mildly. "It's Noah's Ark."

"That's the fun house," Jenny said. "You go in the whale by the side there."

Even in the bright sunshine she felt strange as they walked through the gates. Maybe because it's changed, she told herself. This place really *had* changed. The fun house was the same, but a lot of other things were different.

The old train ride roller coaster was gone, and there was a mine ride called the Pit in its place. There was a new metal coaster called the Steel Demon and a new water ride—the kind where you slosh around in giant inner tubes.

The biggest shock was the new arcade. It was full of shining video games, holograms, virtual reality. Jenny missed the old penny arcade, which had been dark and somewhat spooky, filled with machines from the turn of the century. Ancient, beautifully carved wood and genuine brass—not this steel and neon stuff.

But as time passed, she felt less anxious. She couldn't help it—the park was irresistible. She breathed in the smell of popcorn and ride-grease—and something else, something that was *like* a smell, but wasn't. A cotton-candy feeling of excitement.

"I don't see why Summer would want us to come *here,"* Audrey said when they stopped to buy corn dogs.

"No. I don't think it was a message after all." Jenny was glad to say it. Whatever horrible things they might have to face that night, they could enjoy themselves now.

Michael's blissful corn-dog smile broke up for a moment. "Maybe it's better that way," he said indistinctly. "I'd rather be dead than be what Summer was in that dream."

They went on the roller coasters, screaming, Jenny's loose hair blowing like a banner. The Steel Demon was good, but everyone agreed they liked the creaking, clattering old wooden coasters best. "Scarier," Dee said with relish. "Could break any minute—it *feels* like."

The mine ride was supposed to be scary. "This is a gold mine?" Audrey asked skeptically while lights strobed wildly to simulate dynamite exploding.

"Use your imagination," Michael said, slipping an arm around her.

Jenny looked away. It made her so homesick for Tom that she had to hold her eyes wide open and blinking, willing the tears back where they belonged.

The fun house really *was* scary. A barrel-shaped brick "wall" revolved around them until nobody but Dee could walk straight. The floor shifted and swayed until Michael threatened to sue—or throw up.

"C'mere," Dee said gleefully, beckoning Jenny closer. Behind a glass wall a red figure was vaguely visible. As Jenny stepped up to look, the scene went dark. She leaned forward, her nose almost against the glass—and with a terrible yelling sound the figure swooped straight toward her. It rode down a wire, actually striking the glass. Jenny leaped back with a shriek.

"Good, clean fun," Dee said, chuckling as Jenny leaned against a wall weakly.

Jenny made a fist, but just then something about the red figure caught her eye.

It was a red devil, with horns and split hooves and a tail. But its eyes—its eyes were blue. A blue that shone eerily under the black lights. And just before it was drawn back up the wire—it winked at her.

Jenny's little fingers started to tingle.

After that, things in the park seemed wrong. The barker for the ring-toss game seemed to have an odd gleam in his eye. Even Leo the Paper-Eating Lion seemed vaguely sinister.

"What in the name of God is it?" Michael asked as he sat down heavily on a bench. He was staring at what looked like a car from a circus train, with a red roof and silver bars. Thrust between the bars was a lion's head, muzzle gaping open in a big friendly smile.

"I'm Leo the Paper-Eating Lion!" The voice was

bright and peppy and it came from the muzzle. The timing bothered Jenny; she felt something like the quick cold touch of an ice cube at her neck.

"I eat all kinds of paper," the voice continued joyfully. "I eat cardboard, too. Old gum wrappers, orange peel, popcorn containers. So feed me."

"It's a trash can," Dee explained, squatting to look up the lion's muzzle. "It sucks stuff up like a vacuum cleaner."

A mother wheeled a double stroller up to the car. Both kids stared at the lion with hard expressions.

"Want to feed him?" the mom said.

The kid in front nodded, still unsmiling. She wadded up a paper napkin and threw it at the lion's mouth.

"No, you have to *give* it to him. Here." The mom retrieved the napkin for the kid. The kid, still unsmiling, leaned forward, hand outstretched.

"I bet I'll have a tummyache tomorrow!" Leo caroled.

Forward, forward—the little hand reaching—

"Leo's *always* hungry. . . ."

Jenny jumped up and clapped her hand over the hole in the lion's muzzle just before the kid's fingers got there.

The kid stared at her, never changing expression. The mom squeaked.

"Sorry," Jenny said. *Everyone* was staring at her, even Dee and Audrey and Michael. She didn't move her hand. The kid sat back. The mother, after a flummoxed moment, turned the stroller sharply and wheeled it away.

The back of Jenny's neck was still prickling as she

slowly withdrew her hand. She'd been afraid that—what?

"All right," she said defiantly to the others. "So it was a stupid thing to do. So sue me."

"We're all kind of jumpy—" Michael began soothingly, and then proved it, by ducking as two small figures charged him with a blood-freezing battle yell.

Jenny crouched defensively by the lion before she realized that the two figures were children.

They dived under the wrought-iron bench and came up screaming triumph. "We got it! We got another one!"

"Got what?" Dee said, blocking them with her hightop.

"A doubloon, dummy," the boy said in friendly tones, holding up something round and shining between dirty-nailed fingers. To Jenny, it looked like one of those chocolate candies covered with cheap gold foil. Then he pointed. "Cancha read?"

Jenny twisted her neck. There was a large billboard behind them. Swashbuckling crimson letters announced:

ALL-NEW ATTRACTION! COLLECT THREE GOLD DOUBLOONS AND BE THE FIRST TO SET FOOT ON . . . TREASURE ISLAND.

"You get three tokens and they letcha in free the day it opens. You get to go over the bridge first. They've got 'em hidden all over the park."

Spotting something else interesting, the kids ran away. On the billboard a pirate's treasure chest slowly opened and shut, like a clam's shell. Behind it Jenny could see the central island of Joyland Park, a manmade island in an artificial lagoon. The last time

Jenny had been here, it had been a sort of stage, with acrobatic shows and bands. Now it was clearly under construction, with a tall lighthouse in the middle. She couldn't see any bridge to it.

Why should that make her feel uneasy?

"Just pop those discards in my mouth! Leo's waiting . . ."

"Let's go," Jenny said. Her stomach was churning and she felt she *had* to distract herself. "Let's do something stupid—something *kiddie.* Let's go fishing."

Dark water swirled around and around a channel at the Fish Pond booth. "Like a sushi bar," Michael said, watching the water come in one side and go out the other. "You know, those kinds where the plates float around."

For a quarter you could dip a line into the water. A claw at the end picked up a number and you got a prize.

"When I was a kid all these prizes seemed like treasure," Jenny said. She lowered the claw into the opaque swirl.

"A bite," Dee said. She raised her rod. At the end, dripping, was a wooden bar with a number on it. The attendant glanced at it, then tossed it back into the water. He handed Dee a plastic change purse. Pink.

"Just what I always wanted."

Jenny felt a pull on her line, a sharp tug, almost as if it were a live fish on the hook. She lifted it—

—and gasped.

Oh, God! Oh, *God* . . .

Beside her, Michael's breath hissed in. He was

staring, his chocolate-colored eyes wide and frightened.

There was no wooden bar on the end of Jenny's line. Instead, hanging neatly over one claw of the hook, was a slender, dripping circlet of gold. Jenny didn't need to look at it twice.

It was the ring.

The ring Julian had given her. The one with seven words inscribed on the *inside* of the band, where they would rest against her skin and bind her with their magical power.

All I refuse & thee I chuse. Meaning that Jenny refused all the world and chose—him. A promise that Julian had tried to hold her to. She was free of it, now—but the reminder was chilling.

She'd been wrong about them being able to enjoy themselves until tonight. Julian was watching her this minute, the way he'd watched her for years. There was no getting away from him, not here, not anywhere.

Nothing to do except go and face him.

"Let's go home," Jenny said, surprised at the steadiness of her own voice. She took the ring off the claw and dropped it into the dark, swirling water.

3

"You-uns want the *key?*"

"Well, my parents do. They were kind of jet-lagged so they stayed back at the hotel, you know. They just thought they'd look the place over, you know. Gosh, Mrs. Durash, do you remember that old washing machine that belonged to my great-grandma? And the wringer? That was hysterical, huh, a *wringer.*" I'm being winsome, Jenny realized with a jolt. I'm a con artist.

A smile softened Mrs. Durash's thin features. She was a small woman, slight, wearing what Jenny always remembered her wearing: a print dress and a sweater. "I used to use that washing machine," she said warningly. She pronounced it *warsh*-ing machine.

"I know. That's what's so hysterical!" If I get any cuter, I'm going to throw up, Jenny thought. Oh, Lord—I think I just wrinkled my nose.

But it worked. Mrs. Durash was rummaging in a shiny black purse. "Let me tell you how to turn off the alarm system."

Jenny let out a silent breath of thanksgiving, and listened as intently as she had to the opening instructions of the PSAT. She went down the porch stairs muttering, "Three-six-five-five on the pad, then press Enter, Off, Enter. Three-six-five-five, then Enter . . ."

"We've got a time limit," she added to the others who were waiting around the corner. "The last thing she said was to have my parents call her tomorrow, because she didn't even know we were visiting. When they don't call, she's going to know something's wrong."

"But we didn't get any *sleep,"* Michael pointed out. "And it's a mile back to your grandfather's house. At *least."*

"Let's take a taxi, then," Audrey said impatiently.

"We can't." Dee jingled the fanny pack which contained their pooled funds. "We paid thirteen ninety-five apiece to get into that park, not to mention all the corn dogs Michael ate. We've spent all the money that was supposed to last us for days. We're broke, princess."

"It's my fault," Jenny said after the first horrible moment. "I should have thought. We'll just have to try to get everything done tonight—once we *go,* we won't need to worry about money. Some of us can sleep while the others look through my grandfather's things—we'll take turns, okay? And we can eat some of the Power Bars from the camping stuff we brought."

"But if we don't find it tonight—?"

"We have to," Jenny said. "We'll do it because we *have* to, Michael."

The old brick house still had electricity, presumably to fuel the alarm system. It was spooky inside anyway; furniture draped with white sheets, clocks stopped on the walls. Jenny kept having the same lurching feeling: familiarity—unfamiliarity. Back and forth, or sometimes both at once.

By far the worst was the basement. Jenny's legs didn't want to take her down the stairs. She'd seen this place last month in a sort of dream, a hallucination created by Julian—but she hadn't *really* been here in over ten years. Not since the day neighbors had heard terrible screaming next door and the police had clattered down the stairs to find five-year-old Jenny on the floor, arms scratched, clothes torn, hair a wild yellow tangle. And screaming. Screaming and staring at an open closet door with a strange symbol carved on the front. Screaming in a way that made the biggest policeman *run* back upstairs to call the paramedics.

The police thought her grandfather had done it to her. The scratches, the torn clothes. The blood. They paid no attention at all to the five-year-old's story about ice and shadows in the closet, about hungry eyes that had seen her and tried to take her. About how her grandfather had been taken in her place.

Instead, the police had thought her grandfather had been a lunatic—and just now, looking at the basement, sixteen-year-old Jenny could see why. Every wall, every bookcase, every available surface was jammed with charms of protection.

Not such a bad idea for somebody trying to summon up and trap demons. But, undeniably, it looked weird.

"Will you look at this stuff?" Audrey breathed, enthralled. "Some of it's junk, but I'll bet some of it's priceless. Like this." She stepped forward and lightly touched a silver bell on a shelf. "This is Chinese—I saw these when Daddy was stationed in Hong Kong. You ring them to clear away evil spirits. And that—that's a genuine Tibetan prayer wheel. And this—" She lifted a bracelet of agate and gold beads.

"That's Egyptian," Dee interrupted. "Seven strands, see? Aba says the number seven was sacred to the Egyptians." Dee's grandmother traveled a lot.

"And those are Russian icons," Audrey said, nodding at some gold-plated pictures. "Very rare, very expensive."

"And *that's* from the *Qabalah,"* Michael said, joining the conversation triumphantly and pointing to a chart on the wall labeled *Numerical Values of the Hebrew Alphabet.* "Magical Hebrew divination system."

"A lot of this stuff belongs in a museum," Audrey said.

Jenny was busy trying to breathe. The room was *heavy* somehow—overloaded, oppressive. Stale air mixed with thick, quivering energy.

Magic, I guess, she thought, trying to feel as if she dealt with magical rooms every day. Well, that's what we came for. It's time to start the search.

She made herself go to her grandfather's desk. In her dream of this room—the dream created by Julian—her grandfather's journal had been lying open on the desk. In real life it wasn't so convenient. There was nothing on the desk but a faded green desk pad.

"Maybe on the shelves," she said.

She went to one of the bookcases and tilted her head sideways to read. It had been a brown leather-bound book, and she was sure she would recognize it when she—

"Found it!" she said, darting forward. She opened it to see her grandfather's heavy black handwriting, then looked back at the shelf. "Oh, God, but there isn't just *one* journal. There're three. We'll have to read through them all."

"We'll take turns, like you said." Dee nodded toward the stairway. "You and Michael go up and get some sleep—you're the most tired. Audrey and I can start reading."

Jenny slept for three hours on the living room couch—she couldn't face going into one of the bedrooms—and then went downstairs to take her place beside Michael. She chewed one of Dee's malt-nut Power Bars as she read. She wasn't hungry and she hated the texture of the protein bar, but she knew she needed the energy.

The journals were strange. Her grandfather had written everything up with the precision of a scientist, but what he was writing about was bizarre—and sometimes frightening. Almost all of it dealt with ways to call up the Shadow Men.

The Shadow Men, Jenny thought. Known by different names in different ages: the aliens, the faery folk, the Visitors, the Others. The ones who watched from the shadows and who sometimes took people to—their own place.

Jenny looked up involuntarily at the closet door which stood open, and something like a fist clenched in her gut. That was where they'd taken him. Through that portal into—the other place, the place that existed alongside the human world, always there, never touching. The Shadow World.

Her grandfather had called them up because he wanted their power. But in the end they'd been too powerful for him.

A phrase from the journal caught Jenny's eye. *Walker between the worlds.* Her heart began to pound as she deciphered the dense black writing around it. Something illegible and then *becoming a Walker between the Worlds myself, if the danger wasn't so great. There are several methods to*—something else illegible—*but the one I consider most likely to succeed would be the circle of runes. . . .*

"Runes," Jenny whispered. The magical alphabet that Julian and her grandfather had used to pierce the veil between the worlds. She looked at the drawing below the writing. "Michael, I've got it."

"Really?"

Jenny read a little further and her fingers tightened on the leather cover of the book. "Really. Get Dee and Audrey. And get a knife."

They'd brought Tom's Swiss Army knife, and Dee had a wicked-looking river knife with a five-inch blade. It was meant for rescuing kayakers who needed their ropes cut—quick.

"We have to carve these runes on a door," Jenny

said. "Then we stain them and say their names to charge them with power, and then we open the door."

"Stain them with *what?*" Michael said suspiciously.

"Blood. What else? Don't worry, Michael, I'll take care of it. Let's use the door to the basement—not from the downstairs side, from the other side. It's smooth, good for drawing."

It was funny how simple and everyday it seemed, doing what her grandfather had said he wouldn't try because it was too dangerous. Nobody said, "Are we really going through with this?" Nobody kibitzed—not even Michael. They went about it the same way they'd built the pressed-wood stereo cabinet in Tom's bedroom. Michael read the instructions from the journal aloud; the others followed them.

"Two circles, one inside the other. It doesn't say how big they're supposed to be," Michael said. "But leave room for the runes to go in between them."

Jenny sketched the circles freehand on the smooth oak door with a felt pen.

"Okay, now the runes. First, Dagaz. It goes right at the top and it's shaped like this, like an hourglass on its side," he said. Jenny sketched the angular shape at the top of the inner circle. "It says here that Dagaz is like a catalyst. It represents times like twilight and dawn, when things are just changing. It 'operates between light and darkness.' "

Dawn. Jenny thought about the brilliant blue of the Pennsylvania dawn—and about eyes that were just that color. Julian was like Dagaz, she thought. A catalyst, operating between light and darkness. One foot in either world.

"The next one is Thurisaz, the thorn. It goes to the right—no, a little farther down. It's shaped like—look at this. A straight line with a triangle attached to the side. Like a thorn sticking out of a stem."

"There are a lot of fairy tales about thorns," Audrey said grimly. "You get pricked with a thorn or a spindle or a needle and then you die, or go blind, or you sleep forever."

Silently Jenny drew the rune.

"The next one's Gebo. It stands for a lot of things: a gift, sacrifice, death. The yielding up of the spirit. It's shaped like an *X*, see?"

Sacrifice. Death. A queer shudder went up Jenny's backbone. She stared at the book. It was a straight *X*, not like the slanted *X* of the rune Nauthiz, the one that her grandfather had carved on the closet to restrain the Shadow Men.

"See, Jenny?"

She nodded and drew. But the strange feeling didn't go away. A *bad* feeling—and it was connected with Gebo, somehow. Gebo the rune of sacrifice. Something was going to happen. . . .

Not now. Not right now. In the future.

Michael's voice startled her. "Next is Isa. It's a rune for the power of primal ice. It's just one straight line, up and down."

Jenny tore her mind away from the thought of sacrifice and made herself draw.

"Kenaz, the torch. It's for the power of primal fire, and it's shaped like an angle, see. . . ."

"Raidho, for movement, traveling. Like riding a horse. For protection walking between the worlds. It's shaped like an *R*. . . ."

"Uruz, the ox . . . it's shaped like an upside-down *U*—"

"I know, Michael." Uruz was the rune on the game box that Julian had sold her. "It's supposed to look like ox horns pointing downward, ready to pierce the veil between the worlds," Jenny said. "Is that the last one?"

"Yeah. Now we carve it."

Carving the runes wasn't as hard as Jenny had expected. The door was good thick wood, but the runes were all straight lines and angles, which was much easier to carve than any rounded shape. Still, there were times when Tom's Swiss Army knife stuck or slipped. Jenny was a little frightened of how sharp it was.

And she was worried about the blood. How was she going to do it? She was scared of razor blades, and a pin was out of the question. If they were going to stain all these runes, they'd need a lot more blood than you could squeeze out of a pinprick.

Don't think about it now. When the time comes, you'll just have to use the knife—and hope you don't cut your finger off.

Just then the problem solved itself. The knife slipped.

"God!"

Jenny felt a flash of something, gone almost too quickly to identify as pain. She dropped the knife, and she could feel her eyes widen as she stared at her hand—wondering in that first second how bad it was.

Not bad. A half-inch gash across the meat of her thumb. The lips of the wound showed white before bright red welled up to obscure them. Blood began to slide down her thumb.

Jenny felt just slightly sick. Seeing *inside* your skin—even a little way inside—was disconcerting.

"Quick, use it," Michael said. "Don't waste it—that stuff's precious."

The cut was beginning to sting. Jenny looked around for something to use as a pen, then collected the blood on top of one fingernail and began to trace the runes that were already carved. It stained the pale grooves in the wood a clear light red, the color of a teacher's red ballpoint pen.

Audrey and Dee did the rest of the carving, and Jenny stuck to her gory task. She had to squeeze the cut in the end, but there was enough blood to go around.

The final product of their labors was slightly wobbly but impressive. Two concentric circles, with the runes running between them. Looking at the carving, Jenny wondered for the first time what somebody—a neighbor, say—would think if they caught the kids doing this. Destroying property. Vandalism. As bad as gangs spraypainting graffiti.

Jenny didn't care. She was still operating in crisis mode, in which all normal rules were suspended. She and the others had stepped out of the mainstream, into a place where anything could happen and the only rules were their own. It was scary—and tremendously liberating. Jenny felt as if she were flying toward Tom on wings of fire.

Take him from *me,* will you? she thought to Julian. I don't *think* so. By the time I'm done with you, you'll wish you'd never started this Game.

Dee was regarding the circle critically. "So what now? How does it work?"

"Apparently the idea is that writing runes makes whatever you've written happen," Michael said. "It's like when we drew our nightmares for the first Game, remember? We drew a picture of what we were afraid of, and then our pictures came true. Runes are the same. You make a—a *representation* of something, and it becomes real. You change reality by making the representation."

"That's what Julian told me," Jenny said quietly. "When I put on his ring and said the words, I made my own fate. The words came true when I said them."

"And that's what we have to do with this," Michael said. "We already did the first two steps, carving the runes and staining them. Now all we have to do is charge the runes with power by saying their names out loud. That activates them, and then—"

"And then, look out," Dee said, and her sloe-black eyes flashed. "Let's do it, people."

"We need to get our stuff first," Jenny said. She was trembling-calm now, wrought up to a fine pitch, but determined to do this right, not to jump in without thinking. "We don't know what happens once those runes are activated—we might not have time to do anything then."

They scattered to change their clothes and get things out of their duffel bags. When Jenny came back to the door, she was wearing Levi's and a denim shirt, with a sweater over the shirt and a nylon windbreaker over the sweater. On her feet were thick socks and hiking boots, and at her belt was a bota bag full of water and a pair of leather gloves. A miniature survival kit was in her fanny pack.

Everything in the kit had been chosen for lightness and efficiency. A small waterproof matchbox, a yard of toilet paper, a space rescue blanket folded into a four-inch square. Two heavy-duty plastic bags. Two aspirins. A Hershey Bar. Three tea bags, three bouillon cubes. A string of safety pins. All that was packed in an old tin cup. Tucked in beside the cup were fifty feet of nylon cord, two Power Bars, and a flashlight.

The last thing she put in was Tom's red-handled Swiss Army knife with the six attachments.

They had no idea what they'd be facing in the Shadow World. What kind of terrain, what kind of weather. The glimpse Jenny had gotten through the window of the paper house had shown twisted pinnacles of rock scoured by an endless blizzard and lit by blue and green flashes like lightning. But was the entire world like that?

I'm about to find out, Jenny thought. Very soon. At least this time we're going prepared.

The others arrived, dressed the same way she was. Even Audrey was wearing light hiking boots and a nylon jacket. Dee had tucked the river knife into a black plastic sheath at her belt, but her most deadly weapons were her slender hands and hightop-encased feet.

They all looked at one another, and then, silently, turned to face the door.

Michael gave the book to Jenny. "You should be the one to do it."

Jenny took a deep breath. Holding the journal lightly, she began to read the names.

"Dagaz." *Rune of change.* "Thurisaz." *The thorn.* "Gebo." *For sacrifice.* Jenny's voice was beginning to shake and she couldn't breathe easily. Unconsciously she raised her voice. "Isa." *Primal ice.* "Kenaz." *Primal fire.* The word came out in a staccato burst. "Raidho." *Traveling.* Jenny's throat closed and she lifted her head, looking at the last rune in the circle. A long moment passed.

This is it. This is really it. After I say it, it can't be unsaid. No turning back.

Almost in a whisper she said, "Uruz."

For piercing the veil between the worlds.

With the last word the door began to flash like a strobe light. Black, white, black, white, black, white.

"God!" Audrey said. Everyone jumped a step back. But there was nowhere to go—they were up against the hallway wall. Michael barged into the telephone table and the handset fell off and struck the floor.

In the last month Jenny had seen plenty of bizarre things happen. Julian specialized in the bizarre. But this was different—maybe because the setting was so ordinary, a normal house, a normal door. Or maybe because they'd done it themselves.

And this wasn't just chills-up-the-spine bizarre. This was running-and-screaming bizarre. On Beyond Zebra bizarre.

Within the flashes the circle of runes began to glow like a wheel of fire. Then it started spinning.

Bright as fireworks at midnight—spinning like a Catherine wheel. It was dizzying to look at. Jenny's neck seemed to be frozen, but she looked out of the corner of her eye at the others.

Dee had taken up the Horse stance, in balance without effort, ready for anything. Audrey was flattened against the wall, the fiery light dancing crazily on her auburn hair. Michael's eyes were huge.

A dull roaring began. It seemed to come from the earth itself, vibrating the floor against Jenny's feet.

Oh, God, we did this to ourselves.

Jenny's heart was pounding wildly, out of control. The light was like needles stabbing into her eyes. She was light-headed, half blinded, but she could no longer look away from the wheel.

One final explosion of light—and the roaring became a tearing sound, like a huge tarpaulin ripping in giant hands. It made Jenny want to fall down, curl up, cover her ears.

And then it stopped.

Just like that. One moment agonizing light and deafening, screaming sound—the next moment perfect calm. The door was an oak door again. The wheel of runes was no longer spinning.

But, Jenny saw, it wasn't exactly the way it had been. Dagaz, the rune Jenny had drawn at the top, was now at two o'clock. As if the spinning wheel had overshot slightly before stopping. And the runes burned like sullen coals in the wood.

Jenny was breathing as hard as if she'd just run a race.

"We did it," Dee whispered. Her lips were drawn back from her teeth.

"Did we?" Michael asked huskily.

There was only one way to tell. Jenny gave herself a moment, then slowly reached for the doorknob.

She could feel her pulse in her hand as she grasped the knob. The metal wasn't even warm.

She turned the knob and pulled the door open.

Oh.

Through the open door she could see, not the stairs down to her grandfather's basement, but utter blackness, like a night without stars.

4

Switching on her flashlight, Jenny stepped forward.

There was a resistance as she crossed the threshold. Not like anything solid, more like the g-force she'd felt when the plane accelerated to take off. It made her stumble, not hit the ground quite right.

And the ground seemed to be asphalt. Jenny's flashlight beam made a white circle on it, catching something that looked like a small yellow flower. A smashed flower.

No, not a flower, Jenny realized slowly. The shape was familiar but so far from what she expected to see that she didn't recognize it at first. It was a piece of squashed popcorn.

Popcorn?

Flashlights were switching on behind her, beams crossing and recrossing in the darkness. Dee and Audrey and Michael moved up beside her.

"What the *hell* . . . ?" Dee said.

There was a sound like a door slamming. Jenny

swung her flashlight around just in time to see that it *was* a door slamming, it was the door to her grandfather's basement. She saw it for one instant standing shut, a door with no walls around it, and then it disappeared.

Completely. It was simply gone, leaving them—where they were.

"I don't believe this," Audrey said. The flashlight beams were almost pathetic in the darkness, but they showed Jenny enough.

It was Michael who said it, in tones of shock and indignation.

"It didn't work! After all that—and it's not the Shadow World at all!"

They were in Joyland Park.

It *was* Joyland, exactly as Jenny had seen it that afternoon—except now it was dark and deserted.

The same wrought-iron benches painted green, with smooth wooden planks for backs and seats. The same fences (also green) caging in the same manicured bushes—"poodle bushes," Michael called them. The same pink-and-white begonias Jenny had noticed before—she always noticed flowers. Now their petals were folded tight.

Jenny's flashlight beam caught a heavy-duty brown trash can, an old-fashioned signpost. CANDY CORNER, the signpost read.

The candy store had metal shutters rolled down over its windows and the tiny lights around the signs advertising HOMEMADE FUDGE and CARAMEL APPLES were off.

Jenny just couldn't accept it.

That afternoon the park had been filled with sound: babbling, yelling, ride noises, laughing, music. Now the only sound was her own breath. The motion was the gentle fluttering of pennants at the top of a roller coaster.

Then she noticed something else moving.

On a huge billboard the pirate chest was slowly opening and shutting like a clamshell.

"Nobody's here—not even maintenance people," Dee was saying in dissatisfaction.

"It's too late," Michael said. "They've all gone home."

"But *somebody* should still be here. Look!" Dee's beam flashed across to a little orange cart, nosed up against a fence ahead of them. The cart looked a lot like something a maintenance person might use.

But we didn't see it until after Dee mentioned maintenance people, Jenny thought.

Not just her little fingers but the sides of her hands were beginning to tingle.

There was something wrong here. It *looked* just like Joyland—from the artificial lagoon down to the refreshment cart with the red-and-yellow wheels. But it felt—wrong.

As if something in the darkness was awake and watching them. As if the deserted park around her could come to life at any moment.

"This place is creepy," Audrey announced suddenly.

"Yeah, well." Michael laughed. "Nothing creepier than a closed amusement park."

Words flashed through Jenny's mind. *Did I ever tell you about this amusement park nightmare I had when I was a kid—?"*

"Listen." She turned around abruptly. "Besides Michael, has anybody else had amusement park nightmares?"

Audrey stopped, flashlight drooping. After a moment she said in a subdued voice, "I have."

Dee said quietly, "Me, too."

"And so have I," Jenny said. "Maybe it's one of those universal things—"

"An archetype," Michael interrupted pugnaciously, his voice wobbling slightly. "But so what? That doesn't mean anything. . . ."

Jenny realized then just how bad his dreams must have been.

"Don't be silly, Michael," Audrey said, very gently. She reached out and Michael snuck a finger into her hand. "You think?" she said to Jenny.

"I don't know. It's nothing like I expected. It looks like Joyland, but—"

"But Julian can make anything look like anything," Audrey finished crisply.

Dee looked around, then chuckled. "All right! Listen, you idiots," she said, turning back to them. "This is *good.* If it *is* the Shadow World—or part of it—it's a place we've been. We'll have an advantage, because we know the terrain. And it's better than blue-and-green blizzards, or whatever Jenny saw out that window last time, right?"

Audrey nodded without enthusiasm. Michael didn't move.

"And if it's *not* the Shadow World, we're in real

trouble. Because it means we've blown our chance to find Tom and Zach. Maybe our only chance."

"C'est juste," Audrey said. "I forgot."

Jenny hadn't forgotten. "We'd better check around. See if this is the real Joyland or—" She didn't need to finish the sentence.

She didn't know exactly how they were supposed to tell. The place certainly looked authentic. They crept through the silent park, heading automatically for the front gates, passing a restaurant, dark and still.

"What's that?" Audrey hissed. "I hear something."

It was the sound of water. Faint, coming from up ahead.

"It's the Fish Pond," Jenny said.

She recognized the booth with its red-shingle roof. It was dark, like the other attractions. But when they reached it, she saw that the opaque water was swirling around its circular channel.

"They wouldn't leave that on all night," Audrey said, needle-sharp. "Would they? Would they?"

Jenny's pulse, which had been beating erratically, settled into a slow, heavy thumping.

"You know what, Toto? I don't think we're in Kansas anymore," she whispered.

"Well, well," Dee said, stepping forward. "How about this?"

There was a fishing pole leaning against the booth. Dee hooked an index finger around it.

"Ah. Now. I have a *very* bad feeling about that," Michael said. It was the first time he'd spoken in minutes.

Jenny understood what he meant. It was too obvious, too *inviting.* But they didn't *know* they weren't in Joyland. It was possible that the park might leave the water going at night. Maybe it kept algae from growing or something.

"Shall I?" Dee said, twirling the pole. "Or shall I?"

"You're enjoying yourself, aren't you?" Michael said, and there was something flatly resentful about his voice. "But there's other people here, you know. Whatever trouble you make affects us, too. . . ."

"Oh, come on, you guys. It's the only way to find out, isn't it?"

Jenny chewed her lip. Sometimes Dee's recklessness went out-of-bounds, and nobody but Jenny could stop her. If Jenny didn't say anything, Dee would do it.

Jenny hesitated.

Dee lowered the line into the dark, rushing water.

Jenny realized that she and Audrey and Michael were all braced. None of them was stupid. If this was the Shadow World, something bad would happen. Something *bad.*

The line dangled in the water, slack. Dee jiggled the pole while Jenny thought of all the things that might come up. Dead kittens. Severed hands. Mutant marine life.

Julian knew what you were thinking. He *took* things from your mind and made them real. So if they were in the Shadow World, then the worst thing—the worst thing that any of them was thinking—

"A bite," Dee said. "No, maybe it's just caught."

She leaned over to look, catching the thick yarnlike line in her bare hand and tugging.

"Dee—"

"Come on, come on." Dee tugged, then reached into the water to grope. "What's wrong with—"

"Dee, *don't—*"

Audrey screamed.

The water erupted.

Jenny had seen a geyser once, not Old Faithful, but a smaller one. This looked just the same. There was an explosion of mud-colored water, straight up. It splattered across Jenny's face and beaded on her windbreaker. Then it just *stayed* there, until Jenny suddenly realized that it wasn't water at all, it was something that had come out of the water. Something that had come out and grabbed hold of Dee.

A man—it had hands like a man that were around Dee's throat. But something kept Jenny's brain from recognizing it as a man. In another instant she saw what it was.

The thing had no head.

Its body ended at the shoulders with the stump of a neck. The thing had volition, though, even if it didn't have a brain. It was trying to drag Dee under the water.

All this passed through Jenny's mind in less than a second. Plenty long enough, though, for the thing to wrestle Dee almost to the water's surface.

I'm not brave. I don't know how to fight. But she was grabbing at the thing's arm with both hands. To her horror, her fingernails sank *in,* penetrating the arm beneath the tatter of a sleeve.

It smelled. It smelled *incredibly.* Something terrible had happened to the flesh, turning it into a kind of white, waxy stuff that quivered loosely on its bones.

Like—like that clammy clinging stuff novelty stores use for flesh. Jenny's little brother Joey had a fake snake made out of it. But this creature's flesh was nothing fake. When Jenny involuntarily snatched her hand back, she saw that her nails were full of it.

Everyone was shouting. Somebody was screaming, and after another second Jenny recognized her own voice. With both legs trapped up against the booth and Michael and Audrey hanging on to her, Dee didn't have room to kick. She was fumbling with the knife at her belt.

She got it free and her arm went up—and then Michael yanked her and the wicked-looking river knife fell into the swirling water.

"Her shirt! Her shirt! Her shirt!" Michael was yelling. The body now had Dee by the collar. Michael was trying to pull Dee out of the shirt, but the buttons in front were holding.

Jenny didn't want to touch the headless thing with her bare hands again. She didn't, she didn't—but then the thing wrestled Dee's head almost into the water, and Jenny found herself grabbing its rubbery arm again. It was bent over, dunking Dee's head like someone dunking wash in a river, and Jenny stared directly into its neck-stump. Nothing about its body was nice to look at. What flesh could be seen through the rags of clothes was grotesque—bloated and swollen until it looked like a Kewpie doll that had been boiled and then inflated with a bicycle pump.

The screaming and shouting were still going on. None of their pulling was doing any good. Without conscious thought, Jenny found herself scrambling *over* the wall of the booth, over the channel. One leg dangled in the rushing water, then she was standing in the booth behind the headless thing.

"Pull, Michael! Pull!" Jenny grabbed the thing from behind, arms closing around its waist just above the water level. The waist squashed, like an overripe peach. She could feel things shifting inside the dripping clothes. Her cheek was pressed up against the back of its wet shirt. She locked one of her hands around the opposite wrist and pulled harder.

Oh, God—the *smell.* She opened her mouth to scream again at Michael and gagged instead. She couldn't see anything that was going on in front. All she could do was hang on and keep pulling backward.

The thing seemed to be rooted in the water. She couldn't drag it out. It was a ghastly tug-of-war, with her pulling at the body and Michael and Audrey pulling at Dee. But suddenly she felt something give. The body lurched backward, the tension was gone. Dee was free.

Jenny let go and staggered into the wall of prizes behind her. The thing's arms flailed for a moment, coming in contact with nothing but air. Then, as if something had grabbed its feet and jerked it sharply downward, it disappeared into the dark water.

Everything was silent again.

Jenny was sitting in a litter of plastic whistles, cellophane leis, Matchbox cars, and stuffed koalas. She picked herself up, swaying, and looked over the water channel.

Dee was sprawled almost on Michael's lap. Audrey was half kneeling, half crouching beside them. Everyone was breathing hard.

Dee looked up first. "Jump over quick," she said in the voice of someone who's had strep throat for a week. "I don't think it can see, but it can *feel* when you touch the water."

Jenny jumped over quick, discovering in the process that she'd hurt her ankle sometime, and then all four of them just sat on the asphalt for a while. They were too tired and stunned to talk.

"Whatever it was, it wasn't human," Audrey said at last. "I mean—apart from the head—a human body couldn't look like that."

"Adipocere," Michael got out. "It's what human flesh turns to after a while under water. It's almost like soap. My dad had a mask like that once—he got rid of it because it freaked me out." Michael's father wrote science fiction and had a collection of masks and costumes.

"Then that whole thing was your fault," Dee said unkindly, voice still hoarse. *"Your* nightmare."

Michael, surprisingly, looked hopeful. "You think so? Then maybe I don't have to worry anymore. Maybe the worst's over—for me."

"If your dad had a mask, it wasn't headless, was it?" Jenny said.

"No. What?" Michael looked confused.

"I mean that monster wasn't *exactly* what you had

nightmares about. I think Julian is putting his own little twist on things this time. Besides . . ." Something had been nagging at Jenny since the figure had come shooting up out of the water. A feeling of familiarity. But how could she be familiar with something as monstrous and repulsive as that? Audrey was right, it hadn't even looked human, except that it had two legs and two arms and wore clothes. . . .

Wore *clothes* . . . dank and stinking . . . tattered and dark with water . . . but familiar. A long flannel shirt, black-and-blue plaid, unbuttoned.

"Oh, my *God.* Oh, my God, oh, my God—" Jenny had gotten to her knees, her voice shrill. "Oh, my God, no, it was Slug! Don't you see? It was Slug, it was *Slug* . . ."

She was almost screaming. The others were staring at her with sick horror in their eyes. Slug Martell and P. C. Serrani were the two tough guys who had stolen the paper house from Jenny's living room—and disappeared into the Shadow World. None of Jenny's friends had much sympathy for them, but this . . . nobody deserved this.

"It wasn't Slug," Audrey whispered.

"It was. It *was!*"

"Okay." Dee, eyes wide, scrambled on her knees over to Jenny. She put her arms, slim but hard as a boy's, around Jenny. "Just stay cool."

"No, don't you see?" Jenny's voice was wild and keening. "Don't you *see?* That was Slug, without a head. In Michael's dream he saw Summer's head. What if we find Summer's body, like that? What if we find *Summer?*"

"Damn." Dee pulled back and looked at Jenny. "I know you think it's somehow your fault that Summer died—"

"But what if she's not dead? What if she's wandering around here—" Jenny could feel herself spiraling out of control. She was hyperventilating, hands frozen into claws at chest level.

Dee slapped her.

It was clearly meant to be restorative and it worked, mainly because Jenny was utterly shocked. Dee often threatened physical violence but never, ever used it except in self-defense. Never. Jenny gave a sort of hiccup and stopped having hysterics.

"It's bad," Dee said, her dark eyes with their slightly amber-tinted pupils close to Jenny's and unwavering. "It's really bad, and nobody's saying it isn't." She fingered her throat. "But we have to stay calm, because otherwise we're dead. Obviously we're in the Shadow World—I guess nobody is going to argue about *that*"—she glanced behind her at Audrey and Michael—"and this is some new Game Julian has dreamed up for us. We don't know what to expect, we don't even know the rules. But one thing we do know: If we let it get to us, we're dead before we start. Right?" She shook Jenny a little. "Right?"

Jenny looked into those eyes with their lashes thick as spring grass and black as soot. It was true. Jenny had to get a grip, for the sake of the rest of them. For Tom's sake. She couldn't afford to go crazy right now.

She hiccuped again and unsteadily said, "Right."

"We *all* have to stay calm," Dee said, with another glance at Michael and Audrey. "And we need some weapons. I lost my knife, and if there are any more of those things around . . ."

Jenny realized suddenly that she'd never even thought of getting Tom's Swiss Army knife out of her fanny pack. She wasn't used to fighting. She quickly unzipped the pack and reached in to make sure the knife was safe.

"I've got this," she said, holding it out to Dee.

"Okay, but it's too small. We need something *big* to fight those suckers."

Audrey spoke up in a small, controlled voice. "There were picks and things in the mine ride today. I saw them this afternoon."

"She's right!" Michael said, excited. "They had all those scenes with miners—with axes and shovels and all sorts of stuff. Let's go."

Jenny got up slowly. "I need to get cleaned up first. There's got to be a bathroom around here somewhere." Her jeans were wet from the channel water, but even worse was the stinking ooze on her windbreaker and hands.

There was a bathroom beside the restaurant, and it was open. Jenny washed her jeans as best she could. The windbreaker she threw in the trash, along with her damp sweater. She washed her hands and face over and over and then stood under the blower trying to dry her shirt and jeans.

She and Dee guarded the rest room entrance while Michael and Audrey took their turn washing, and Jenny noticed a squashed cigarette butt on the ground. She stared at it for several minutes, the night breeze cool on her damp jeans. Every detail, she thought. Julian must have re-created everything in the real park, making it realistic down to the tiniest detail.

Which didn't mean there weren't nasty, unrealistic surprises around any given corner. They'd only been here half an hour, and already one of them had nearly died. On his own ground Julian's illusions were real—or real enough that no amount of disbelief would shake them. In the Shadow World he was the master. Jenny had the feeling that all her worst amusement park nightmares were about to come true.

And we haven't even *seen* Julian yet, she thought. He's got to be here, somewhere, laughing himself sick at us.

As they set off for the mine ride, Audrey said, "I hear music."

5

The music seemed to be coming from a distant corner of the park—somewhere in back, maybe near the arcade. For an instant Jenny saw lights glimmering through the trees. But the rides they passed were dark and still. The bumper cars were motionless humps like frozen cattle, and Jenny got a whiff of the graphite that kept the metal floor slippery.

What is it about amusement parks? she wondered as the bulk of a roller coaster blotted out the stars. What makes them give people nightmares?

It's because there's something mystical about them, she thought. About some of them, anyway—not the really new, totally sanitized, Hallmark-Pepsi-Colgate kind, but some of the older ones, or the ones that had older sections. In some of those there was something mystical, ancient—significant. Something more than met the eye.

The lights twinkled like will-o'-the-wisps up ahead, but Jenny and the others never seemed to get any closer to them. The music was so faint that she couldn't make out the tune.

Then she heard a new sound, a *slap-pad, slap-pad* like quick bare footsteps. Dee whirled instantly to face it. Jenny clutched Tom's knife. An hour ago she would have been afraid to walk around with it open—it was *sharp*—and now she was afraid to close it.

Four flashlights swept the manicured shrubbery, illuminating nothing more sinister than a clock made of flowers. Then Michael shouted, "There!"

Something was scampering across a path on the other side of the shrubbery. The flashlights picked out a slate-colored figure. It was moving too fast for Jenny to get a good look at it, but her impression was of something very small and impossibly deformed. Something like a withered gray fetus.

It disappeared behind—or into—the Whip.

"Should we go after it?" Dee asked.

Dee was *asking?* She must be half dead, Jenny thought. She said, "No. It's not bothering us, and we're not armed yet." It gave her a vaguely military and important feeling to say *armed.* "Let's get to the mine ride first."

"But what was it?" Audrey said.

"It looked like a monkey," said Michael.

"It was little," Jenny said—and then she thought of something. Her dream. The little man in the elevator, the man with the mask.

Can we take you? We can carry you.

The Shadow Men might ask something like that—but that wizened thing couldn't have been a Shadow

Man. The Shadow Men were beautiful, frighteningly and heartbreakingly beautiful.

"Whatever it was, we'd better watch our backs," Dee said. "There might be more of them."

The mine ride was as dark as everything else. Jenny shined her flashlight on the freestanding control box with its little lights and switches.

"We don't have to *use* that, do we?" Michael said.

"No, I don't think so," said Jenny. She glanced behind her at the miniature train that stood waiting by the loading platform, then turned her flashlight on the track. "I think the train runs on its own power—see how the track looks just like a regular train track?—but it doesn't matter. I think we should walk."

Audrey opened her mouth as if to protest, then shut it again. All four flashlights converged on the mouth of the "cave" where the track disappeared. In the ordinary park this cave was a dark and fanciful gold mine full of ghostly miners, flooded shafts, skeletons, bats, and dynamite. In the Shadow Park, it might hold anything.

"Let's do it," Jenny said.

Going into the cave was like being swallowed. As they walked slowly along the track, Jenny glanced back and saw a circle of lighter black behind them—the outside world, getting smaller and smaller.

At about this point in the ordinary ride there had been colored lights and mist around the train, probably meant to show you were going back in time to gold mining days. Tonight, there was just a musty damp smell.

There were no lights to illuminate the scenes in the cave, either, and it gave Jenny a jolt when her flashlight caught a figure in the shadows. It was a mustached miner with rolled-up sleeves, loading dynamite into a hole in the rock while two other miners watched.

"That one's holding a sledgehammer," Dee said.

"Yeah, but it's way too heavy. None of us could even pick it up," Jenny said. "We'd better see what's farther down. I do remember pickaxes and things."

"We can't get lost as long as we follow the track," Michael added. Jenny noticed he seemed almost cheerful now.

Dee shrugged and they went on. The next scene showed what happened after the dynamite went off—a cave-in that left the three miners trapped beneath a wall of boulders. In the ordinary ride there had been screams and moans of "Let me out!" and "Help me!" It was almost scarier without the sound effects, Jenny thought. The figures in the boulders were scary as waxworks, while the flashlights made shadows leap on the cave wall behind them. Jenny found herself staring at one clawed hand reaching above the tumbled rocks.

"Are they moving?"

"It's your hand shaking," Audrey said in an edged voice.

"It's all just papier-mâché," Michael said and thumped the cave wall. It sounded like hitting a surfboard. "Ow. I lied. It's fiberglass."

There were more scenes: a flooded shaft with real water, a hanging, even a wilderness saloon with skeletons as patrons. They climbed up to examine the saloon.

"These bottles might work," Dee said, taking one from a bony hand. Strange, Jenny realized—the bottle didn't look like modern glass. It was thick and milky with age and it said CROWN DISTILLERIES CO. on the front.

All the bottles looked old. They were brown, dark blue, green, even pink, and they bore imprints like AVEN HOBOKEN & CO. and PEARSON'S SODAWORKS.

"Very authentic," she said. "I didn't think Joyland took so much trouble."

The others exchanged glances, but said nothing.

"We'd better keep looking," Jenny added.

They passed another trapped miner, this one with thousands of small black ants crawling over his face. Jenny was liking the figures less and less—the feeling that they might start moving at any minute was almost unbearable. They passed strange waterfalls where purple water flowed like glass down broad steps of rock into a colored pool.

"There!" Dee said as they rounded a corner. "Picks!"

Miners were standing around a stream, leaning on shovels or holding pickaxes. Several had Bowie knives or pistols thrust through their belts.

Dee was already boosting herself up into the scene. "Look at this, it's great!" It was a tool with a wooden handle as long as a yardstick and an iron head. Neither side of the head was very sharp. One ended in a sort of blunt spike as long as Jenny's little finger; the other was flat and triangular. For scooping? Jenny wondered.

Dee was moving the tool up and down, trying to get it out of the miner's loose grasp. The miner, hat brim drooping wearily, stood impassive.

"Here's one I like," Audrey said grimly. She'd found a pick that was sharp on both sides.

Dee shook her head. "Too flimsy. See how the head's just tied on to the handle with rawhide? It might not hold." She succeeded in prying the tall pick loose and held it up triumphantly. "Now *this* is a weapon."

Michael was holding up an iron forklike thing with six heavy, curved tines. *"Nightmare on Elm Street,"* he said.

Jenny put the Swiss Army knife in her pocket, gripped her flashlight in her teeth, and wrestled free a tool of her own. It had a short wooden handle and an iron head with a five-inch-long projection. She couldn't tell if it was a hammer or a pick, but it felt good in her hand, and she swung it once or twice for practice.

That was why she wasn't sure if the ground really moved a moment later, or if she was just off balance. She stopped swinging.

"Did anybody feel that?"

Dee was looking at the platform they were all standing on. "I don't think this thing is too stable."

"I didn't feel anything," Michael said.

Jenny felt a flicker of apprehension. Maybe it was just the platform—or maybe she was just dizzy—but she thought it was time to get out of there.

"Let's go back."

"You got it, Sunshine," Dee said, swinging the pick onto her shoulder. They all scrambled down, knocking ornamental gravel onto the track with a sound like popcorn in a pan.

"Follow the yellow brick road," Michael said, waving his flashlight beam along the track.

And we can't get lost, Jenny completed the thought in her mind. We can't. We'll be fine.

So why did she have a cold knot in her stomach?

Michael, at the front, was now humming "I've been working on the railroad." Suddenly his flashlight stopped swinging.

"Hey. What the—*hey!"*

Jenny sucked in her breath, feeling her chest tighten even as she pushed her way past Audrey.

Michael was sputtering indignantly, staring down at his feet. Jenny saw the problem immediately.

The railroad tracks split.

"Did they do this before?" Jenny swept her flashlight beam first one way, then the other. Both sides were the same: metal rails laid over thick wooden boards. But they went in different directions.

"No. They never split. I would have noticed," Dee said positively.

Audrey let her pick down with a solid thump. "But it wouldn't have looked like a split from our direction. It would have been two tracks joining."

"Splitting, joining, it doesn't matter. I'd have noticed."

"But it would have been behind us. In the dark—"

"I would have noticed!"

"Hey, guys, guys—" Michael began, making the time-out sign with his fork and flashlight. It was completely ineffectual. "Guys—"

"I am not a guy," Audrey snapped and turned

back on Dee. It didn't matter what the argument was about anymore, it was turning into another Dee-Audrey jihad.

"Oh, fine, yell at me, too—" Michael began.

"Shut the hell up—*all of you!*" Jenny shouted.

Startled, everyone shut up.

"Are you people crazy? We don't have time to argue. We don't have time for anything. Maybe the track split before and maybe it didn't, but we came up by *that* wall." She pointed to her right. "We'll go that way and it should take us out."

Except, she thought, that nothing is what it should be when Julian's involved. And that tremor she'd felt before—maybe the ground really had moved.

The others, looking as if a summer thunderstorm had come and gone in their midst, meekly set out in the direction she'd indicated. But Dee said quietly, "If we *are* going the right way, we should see that miner with the ants all over him pretty soon."

They didn't.

The knot in Jenny's stomach pulled tighter and tighter. The right-hand wall was blank—and it seemed to be closing in. This place was looking less like a tunnel for a train ride and more like a real mine shaft all the time.

It was almost a relief to finally run into the proof. She rounded a slight curve and saw an ore car sitting squarely on the track in front of her.

A real ore car—at least as far as Jenny could tell. It was four or five feet long with rounded corners and solid wheels set close together under its center. It smelled like rusty iron—like a witch's cauldron,

Jenny thought—and echoed slightly when she spoke while bending over it.

"This isn't part of the ride," she said.

"It would be stupid of a park to leave it here," Dee said and tried to pull it by the hitch in front. It clanged, but didn't move far.

Jenny had a wild impulse to jump into it and stay there.

She looked up slowly at the others.

Michael's flashlight lit up Audrey's hair from behind, giving her a copper halo. Dee was just a slim black shadow at Jenny's side. Jenny didn't need to see their faces to know what they were feeling.

"Okay, so we're in trouble," she said. "We should have known, really. So whose nightmare is this?"

The slim black shadow showed a glimmer of white teeth. "Mine, I guess. I'm not in love with enclosed spaces."

Jenny was surprised. The last time they'd been down in a cavern, she hadn't noticed Dee having any problems—but then, the last time her attention had been focused pretty exclusively on Audrey.

"I'm just a *little* claustrophobic. I mean, I don't remember having any dreams about this kind of thing. But"—Dee let out a breath—"I guess if you asked me what's the worst way to die, I'd have to say a cave-in would rank right up there."

"God, do we have to worry about *that?* Horrible ways to die?" Michael exploded. "I could fill a book."

"What am I most afraid of, I wonder?" Audrey said, rather emotionlessly. "Pain? A lot of pain?"

Jenny didn't want to think about it. "We've got to go back and follow the tracks the other way. It's our only chance."

They were headed deeper into the mine now. The hammer bounced bruisingly on Jenny's shoulder.

Since they were retracing their steps, the shaft should have opened up again. But it didn't. The walls closed in until Jenny could have touched irregular outcrops with her fingertips. The ceiling got lower and lower until it brushed Jenny's hair.

She gathered the flashlight and hammer in one hand so she could touch the cavern wall with the other. "Definitely not fiberglass," she murmured.

Not fiberglass but rock—and surprisingly beautiful rock. She could see veins of milky white and orange, the orange ranging from palest apricot to a rusty burnt sienna. It all sparkled with millions of infinitesimal pinpricks of quartz.

"Ore," Michael said. "You know, the kind gold comes in."

"This park was built on a coal mine," Jenny said. "They mined coal everywhere around here—but that was back in the eighteen hundreds."

"Different kind of mine," Michael said. "This is a real gold mine we're in."

Rock was everywhere—very rough, maybe carved but looking natural because it was so irregular. It was like being in a castle, Jenny decided.

And it was *cold.* She wished she hadn't thrown her sweater away.

Dee, a step ahead, was walking with her shoulders drawn in. Jenny could sympathize. She was beginning to feel the pressure of the rock around her—the solidity of it. They were in an endless buried shaft of orange and brown and black.

When the first junction came, everyone stopped.

"The tracks go straight," Jenny said. She knew perfectly well that that didn't mean anything. This wasn't the split in the tracks they'd seen before. A long corridor simply stretched out into the darkness on one side.

They followed the tracks straight ahead.

The stripes of white on the walls got bigger and bigger the farther they went. It was damp, now, and the walls felt icy and dirty. When Jenny touched them, her fingers came away black.

They came to a place where the roof opened into a sudden cavern—a horizontal shaft maybe thirty feet up. Jenny could see a vein of rust-colored rock at the top, and below that gray slate ridged and grooved as if water had flowed down it.

"That shaft or cavern or whatever goes back a way," Dee said. "We could maybe climb it. . . ."

"Or maybe not," Jenny said. She understood why Dee wanted to get out of the lower tunnel, but she didn't like the look of that black hole up there. "We'd break our necks, and there could be anything—or anybody—up there."

Audrey said, "Well, it's obvious that things are changing around us. I was wrong about the track, Dee."

Dee gave her a startled look. She wasn't used to apologies from Audrey.

Something cold struck Jenny's cheek. She touched

it and felt wetness—and then another drop on her hair.

"Listen," Michael said.

At first Jenny didn't hear anything. Then it came, the loneliest sound in the world. Water dripping musically onto rock—slow drops that seemed to echo through the deserted shafts. It sounded far away.

"Oh, God," Jenny whispered illogically, "we really are lost." The lonely dripping brought it all home. They were trapped under tons of rock, in the dark, far from any help, and with no idea of where to go.

Dee said, "Uh-oh," and then stopped.

"What? *What?*"

"Well—I just remembered a nightmare I had once about a cave."

"It didn't flood, did it?" Jenny asked, thinking of the miners in the scene on the train ride.

"No. It just sort of collapsed."

Audrey said, "I don't think we should be *talking* about this. *Tu comprend?*"

She was right, of course. They shouldn't be talking, or thinking, or anything. Blank minds were what they needed. But Jenny's mind was out of control, following Dee's words like a spark running down a fuse.

"On you?" she said. "Did it collapse on you? Or were you just trapped—"

That was as far as she got before the ground started to rumble. Only it wasn't just the ground, it was the ceiling, the walls, everything.

"Which way?" Dee cried, as good in a pinch as

always, even if this was her nightmare. She swung her flashlight around, looking up and down the shaft. "Where's it coming from?"

Jenny saw rocks falling from the vertical shaft behind them. Michael's flashlight was on the same thing.

"Come on!" he shouted, starting the other way. "Come on! Come on!"

"It's all coming down!" Audrey shouted.

"Come on! Come on!" Michael just kept yelling it, his voice higher and higher.

The floor was rocking—like the tremor Jenny had felt earlier, only much, much bigger. She couldn't see anything clearly. Flashlights were waving all over the place.

"We can't go that way—"

"Watch out—the *rock—* "

Above the shouting voices was the voice of the rock, a grinding, shuddering, smashing sound. Jenny was trying to run, bruising herself on outcrops that seemed to jump into her path. She was being thrown from side to side.

"The floor—!"

She heard Audrey's shriek, but was too late to stop herself. There was a gap in the floor of the shaft, a vertical cavern down to another shaft. Small rocks were falling into it, and Jenny's flashlight illuminated dust particles swirling madly in the air. Then she was falling, too.

The first blow hurt, but after that she was in shock and just bounced off the outcrops numbly. She felt her fanny pack tear free. Her hammer and flashlight were already gone, along with the bota bag. Then she was rolling and sliding, part of an avalanche that carried her with it effortlessly.

Then the noise and confusion receded and her mind went blank.

She was alone, in complete darkness and utter silence. Her throat was full of choking dust. And she was terrified.

Jenny knew this before she remembered who she was or how she'd gotten there. It was one of those terrible awakenings—like the kind she used to have in the middle of the night, when she jerked out of sleep *knowing* that something was out there in the dark, and that it was bad. And that in the daytime she would forget all about it again.

The worst thing was that this wasn't a dream. There was no bedside light to turn on, no parents to run to. Instead there was only darkness and the sound of her own breathing.

"Dee!" The shout came out pathetically weak. And it didn't echo properly. Jenny turned her face up but couldn't feel the slightest air current.

She was in an enclosed place. The rock must have blocked up the entrance she'd fallen through.

"Dee! Audrey!" Oh, worse than pathetic. Her voice died out completely in the middle of "Michael!"

Then she sat perfectly still, listening.

If I don't move, it won't get me.

That was ridiculous, of course. It only worked for monsters under the bed. But all her muscles were locked, so tense they were shaking.

She couldn't hear a sound. Not even a faint after-rumble from the cave-in. The darkness folded on itself around her.

She felt herself begin to panic.

Oh, please, no . . . just keep calm, think of something . . . but I'm *scared.* There must be some way out . . . you can move around, see what this place is like.

But she couldn't. She couldn't move. It was too dark. She could feel her eyes widening and widening, useless as the blind bumps on white cave fish.

Anything could be out there—coming at me—from any direction . . .

The panic was now a riot. She was utterly terrified that she *would* hear a noise, a noise of something approaching in the blackness.

But I fell in alone. This is a small place; I can feel it. I'm alone. Nothing's here with me. Nothing can get in. Nothing—

Rock scraped lightly on rock.

Jenny twisted to face it, still kneeling. The faint sound was lost now because her heart was going like a trip-hammer and her ears were ringing with sheer terror.

Oh, God—

"Ragnarok," said a musical voice, "means both a rain of dust and the end of the world. To the people who discovered the runes, I mean. Don't you think that's interesting?"

6

Julian . . ." The sensation was exactly like falling down the mine shaft.

Then she said sharply, "Where are you?"

"Here." Red light blossomed.

Jenny tried, in the moment before her eyes adjusted, to brace herself. But she could never brace for Julian—he was as much a shock to her senses as ever.

A beautiful shock, like a completely unexpected riff in a dull jazz piece. Like a picture you could pore over for hours and still find new and startling details in. Everything about him was so perfect and so perfectly outrageous that your eye darted from feature to feature in dazzled confusion.

Just now the red light glinted off his hair like fire on snow. It turned his impossibly blue eyes to an equally impossible violet. It threw dancing shadows across the planes of his face, bringing into relief the sculpted beauty of his upper lip. It cast an unholy glow all around him—which was entirely appropriate, because Julian was as seductive as mortal sin and as haughty as the devil.

He was wearing black like a second skin, pants and vest without a shirt. The red light came from the torch he was holding.

Jenny, devastatingly aware that her jeans were crunchy from drying wrinkled and her denim shirt looked as if she'd crawled through a chimney, said, "You invited me to come—and here I am."

He answered as easily as if they'd been talking for hours. "Yes, and you're off to a bad start. Couldn't even avoid this simple trap. Don't even know what game you're playing."

"Whatever it is, it's the last Game," Jenny said.

It wasn't the same as it had been before, when she'd felt as if she were fighting him all the time in her mind—whether he was physically present or not. Fighting his sensuality, fighting his beauty, fighting the memory of his touch.

In those days part of her actually longed for the moment when she would stop fighting, for the final surrender. But now . . .

Jenny had changed. The fire she'd passed through in the last Game, the one he'd created to trap her, had changed her. It had burned away the part of her that had responded to Julian, that had craved his danger and wildness. Jenny had come through the fire alive—and purified. She might not be as powerful as Julian, but her will was as strong as his.

She would *never* give in to the shadows again. And

that meant that everything was different between them.

She could see that he saw the difference. He said, "More light?" and made a gesture, like tracing a line in the air.

Kenaz, Jenny thought. The rune of the torch, one of the runes she'd carved on her grandfather's oak door. It was shaped like an acute angle, like a lesser-than sign in mathematics. When Julian's long fingers made the gesture, the light seemed to ripple, and with a magician's flourish he plucked a second burning torch from the air.

Jenny, stony-faced, clapped her hands two or three times.

Julian's glance was blue as a gas flame. "You don't want to get me angry. Not this early on," he said with dangerous quietness.

"I thought I was supposed to be impressed."

He studied her. "You *really* don't want to get me angry."

Oh, he was gorgeous, all right. Inhuman, incomprehensible, and so alive he looked as if he should be dripping fire or electricity from his fingertips. He brought a shine with him like diamonds in coal. But Jenny had a core of steel.

"Where's Tom?" she said.

"You haven't been thinking about him," said Julian.

It was true. Jenny hadn't. Not continuously, not constantly, the way she had in the old days when she'd never really regarded herself as a separate person, but as part of a unit: Tom-and-Jenny. It didn't matter.

"I came here for him," she said. "I don't need to think about him every minute to love him. I want him back."

"Then win the Game." Julian's voice was as cold and ominous as thin ice breaking.

He stuck one torch into a wide horizontal crack in the wall. Jenny hadn't really taken in her surroundings yet—when Julian was around it was very difficult to focus on anything except him—but she saw now that she'd been right in her guess earlier. This was an enclosed place, and a very small one, scarcely as big as her bedroom at home. Three of its walls were stone; the fourth was solidly packed boulders.

Below the crack with the torch was a sort of natural stairway, each step broader than the one above it. Like the fake waterfalls in the mine ride, Jenny thought, only without the water. She noticed her flashlight, apparently dead, lying by the bottom step.

There was no entrance or exit to the room. The ceiling was low. It had a very *trapped* feeling about it.

Jenny's heart sank a little.

No. Don't you dare let him frighten you. That's what he wants, that's what kicks him.

Besides, what's to be scared of? So you're buried alive under tons of rock, alone with a demon prince who wants you body and soul and will literally do anything to have you. Who might kill you just to make sure no one *else* can have you. And you're pissing him off deliberately, but so what, why sweat the details?

She tried to make her voice quite steady and a

little blasé as she said, "So just what is the Game this time?"

"The clue will cost you."

Icy fury swept over Jenny. "You're horrible. Do you know that?"

"I'm as cruel as life," Julian said. "As cruel as love."

The fury, and the steel at Jenny's core, gave her the courage to do something that astonished even her. She wanted to slap Julian. Instead, she kissed him.

It wasn't like the tender, cozy sort of kiss she gave Tom, and not like the terrified, half-wild kisses Julian had extorted from her in the old days, either. She jumped up and snatched his face between her palms before he could do anything with the torch. She kissed him hard, aggressively, and without the slightest vestige of maidenly shyness.

She felt his shock. His free hand came up around her, but he couldn't pull her any closer than she was already pressing herself. She ignored the danger of the torch completely—if it was close to her hair, that was Julian's problem. Let the great master of the elements figure it out.

Julian recovered fast. It was possible to take him off guard, but he didn't stay nonplussed long. Jenny felt him trying to take control of the situation, trying to soften the kiss.

But she knew the danger of softness. Julian could spin a web of shadows around you, with touches like the brush of moth's wings and kisses soft as twilight. He could turn your own senses against you until the kisses left you dizzy and breathless and the moth's-wing touches put you on slow burn. And by the time you realized what was underneath the softness, you were shivering and melting and lost.

So Jenny kept this kiss strictly business. A cheap and nasty sort of business she'd never had to do before because before Julian she'd only ever kissed Tom. She kissed him angrily, with a clinical coldness and all the expertise she could muster. At the end she realized she'd managed to startle him twice in just a matter of minutes. When she pulled away—which she did easily—she could see the shock in his eyes.

Didn't think I could resist, did you? she thought. She stepped back and with utter coldness said, "Now, what about my clue?"

Julian stared. Then he laughed mockingly, but she could see him losing his temper, see the blue eyes glitter with rage like exotic sapphires. She had struck at his pride—and hit dead center.

"Well, now, I'm not sure I got my money's worth," he said. "I've known icicles that were better kissers than that."

"And I've known dead fish that were better kissers than you," Jenny said—untruthfully and with an insane disregard for danger. She *knew* it was insane, but she didn't care. The freedom of knowing that the shadows had no power over her was intoxicating. It made this encounter with Julian different from any other.

She'd struck home again. She saw the menacing fury well up in his eyes—and then his heavy lashes drooped, veiling them. A half smile curved his lips.

Jenny's stomach lurched.

He was evil, she knew. Cruel, capricious, and dangerous as a cobra. And she'd been stupid to goad him that way, because right now he was planning something bad—or her name wasn't Jenny Lint-for-Brains Thornton.

"I'll give you your clue," he said. He slid a hand into one skintight pocket and brought it out again, flipping something gold on his thumb and catching it again. The gold thing winked in the torchlight, up and down. "Heads I win, tails you lose," Julian said and gave her a smile of terrible sweetness.

Then he flicked the shining gold thing at her so quickly that she flinched. It hit the stone with a wonderful clear ringing clink. Jenny picked it up and found that it was cold and quite heavy. It was a coin, round but irregular, like a very thin home-baked cookie.

"A Spanish doubloon," Julian said, but even then she stared at him a moment before getting it.

Oh, God—of course. The game—the one the real Joyland Park was holding. What had that kid said this afternoon? *"You get three tokens and they let you in free. . . ."* And the billboard: COLLECT THREE GOLD DOUBLOONS AND BE THE FIRST TO SET FOOT ON . . . TREASURE ISLAND.

And Julian had invited them to come on a treasure hunt. But Jenny hadn't made the connection, not even when that giant treasure chest had been the only thing moving in the park tonight.

"You modeled this whole place after Joyland because they were having a treasure hunt? Why? Because I used to go to the park when I was a kid?"

He laughed. "Don't flatter yourself. This whole—Shadow Park, if you like—already existed. It was created ten years ago and for a very different reason.

A special reason . . . but you'll find out about that later." He gave a strange smile that sent a chill through Jenny. "It was built on an old coal mine, you know—a pit. The Shadow Men have been here a long time."

A pit. *Deep into the Pit,* Jenny remembered. That was a line from the poem she'd found on her grandfather's desk in Julian's first Game. Was that how her grandfather had found the Shadow Men in the first place? Had he taken a question deep into a pit, into some place where the worlds were connected?

She would probably never know—unless Julian told her, which didn't seem likely. But it cast a vaguely sinister light over the real Joyland Park.

Forget the conjectural crap, she told herself. Get down to business.

"Tom and Zach are on Treasure Island," she said.

She got a wolfish smile back. "Right. And don't even think about trying to swim there or anything. The bridge is the only way, and the toll is three gold doubloons. You'll find the coins hidden throughout the park."

"I've got one already," she reminded him, closing her fist on the coin.

His smile turned dreamy, which was even more frightening than the wolf look. "Yes, you do, don't you?" he said pleasantly. "Now all you have to do is get out with it."

On the word *it,* everything went dark.

It happened so fast that it took Jenny's breath away. One moment she was conversing by the light of two ruddy torches, the next she was in pitch blackness. Blackness so profound that it made her heart jump and her eyes fly open. She saw ghostly blue pinwheels, then nothing. It was like being struck blind.

Okay. Don't panic. He made a mistake—he got mad and screwed up. He left the flashlight.

I hope, her mind added, as she stuck the doubloon in her pocket and cautiously felt her way in the darkness.

Her hand closed around cold metal. She held her breath and thumbed the switch.

Light. Only a tiny light, a dull orange-ish glow. Either something had happened to the flashlight in the fall or the batteries were going dead. But it was enough to keep her from going crazy.

You shouldn't have made him mad, Jenny. That was really, really dumb.

Because, even with light, she was in trouble. By holding the flashlight very close she could see the rock walls of her prison quite clearly. She could examine every inch of it, from the low ceiling, to the uneven floor, to the solidly packed boulders that blocked the entrance.

There was no way in or out. She couldn't possibly shift those boulders by herself—and if she did move one, she'd probably bring the rest of them down on top of her.

Don't panic. Don't, don't, don't panic.

But the flashlight was already getting dimmer. She could see it, but not anything around it. And she was alone in the midst of solid rock and absolute silence. There was no sound, not even the drip of water.

Wait. You thought your way out of a fire in the last

Game—why not a cave now? Come on, try. Just imagine the rock wall melting, imagine your hand moving through it. . . .

But it didn't work. As she'd suspected before, here in the Shadow World, Julian's illusions were too strong to be broken. He was the master here.

Which meant she was stuck, unless someone came to help her.

Okay, then. Yelling time.

She made herself shout. And again, and again. She even picked up a fist-size rock that lay at the bottom of the pile and banged on each stone wall, slowly and rhythmically. In between each burst of noise, she listened.

There was absolutely no sound in answer.

At last, with the flashlight nearly out, she sat down with her back against the boulders, drawing her arms and legs in like an anemone.

Then the whispering began.

It started so softly that at first she thought it might be the blood rushing in her ears. But it was real. The voices were distant and musical—and menacing. What they were saying was too indistinct to be made out.

Shoulders hunched, Jenny turned her head slowly, trying to locate the sound. And there, in the darkness, she saw eyes.

They glowed with their own light, like foxfire. They were cold, ravenous. She recognized them from her grandfather's closet.

The Shadow Men. The Shadow Men were here with her.

Their eyes seemed to stare out of the wall itself.

They were *in* the rock, somehow. Jenny felt the hairs on her arms erect, felt a prickling that ran from her little fingers to her palms and all the way up to her elbows. A primitive reaction to what she saw in front of her.

Everyone, everywhere, knew about the eyes, she thought. Underneath, everybody really knew, even though people tried to suppress the knowledge in the daytime. At night sometimes the knowledge burst out—the sense of watching eyes that shared the world with humans. Eyes that were ancient and infinitely malevolent and that had no more concept of pity than a wasp or a T. Rex.

Except that they were gifted with intelligence—maybe more intelligence than humans. Which made them doubly terrifying.

And they want you terrified, Jenny. So just keep your head. They're here to scare you, but they won't do anything to you.

But they're whispering. . . .

Such a juvenile thing. They were whispering gibberish—and it frightened her sick. Distorted, unnatural sounds. Like records played backward, at low speed.

She couldn't help listening and trying to make sense of it—even while she was terrified of doing just that. She didn't *want* the gibberish to make sense.

Then, to her surprise and vast relief, the eyes went out.

They didn't fade away as much as seem to recede across some great distance. The voices lingered for a moment and then died.

Thank you, Jenny thought fervently, leaning her bent head on her knees. Oh, thank you. The silence seemed almost welcome now.

Then she heard another sound, a liquid rippling that the hissing voices had obscured. She turned the dying flashlight toward the wall with the steps, where the eyes had been. Then she jumped up with a gasp and brought it closer.

The steps—were moving. No. As she brought the flashlight right up to the wall she felt a splash of wetness against her hand. The steps weren't moving, they were just covered with water.

Water was flowing down the rock staircase, smooth as glass. Just like the waterfalls in the mine ride.

Only faster. It was pouring in a steady sheet all along the width of the crack—maybe three or four feet. It was flooding out like a hotel fountain.

Strangely, it seemed just an inconvenience at first, and not nearly as scary as the eyes had been. Jenny didn't recognize it as a danger until her feet were soaked.

It's not flowing out through the boulders, she realized slowly. Weird. They must be *really* packed to be sealed. Or maybe there's just a blank wall behind them and only the ceiling was open when I fell through. But now even the ceiling's blocked up.

And that water's still coming. . . .

It was coming, and faster every minute, and icy cold. Her feet were actually numb inside her hiking boots. Too bad I lost the fanny pack—I had those Baggies for wading, she thought, and then she realized that she was going to die.

This was a sealed cavern. Sealed. Smaller than her bedroom and filling up faster than her dad's swimming pool. The water was going to come in and in—

—and where will the air go? she wondered, stumped for a moment by this problem in physics. For a moment she thought she was saved. If the air couldn't get out, no more water could get in.

But there was probably room for the air to go out the ceiling, beyond the boulders somewhere. Up in some place Jenny couldn't find because the flashlight was completely dead now. She was standing in darkness, with water rising around her calves, and if she tried to climb those boulders blindly and pull at them, they would crush her. And if she didn't, she would eventually be left with her mouth up against the ceiling, gasping for the last tiny breath of air before the water took her.

She wasn't hysterical, but thoughts were rushing through her mind with dizzying speed. She was remembering the flooded-cavern scene in the mine ride above, and the clawed hand reaching above the boulders. And she thought she knew what some of the whispering voices had been saying.

"Die . . . die . . ."

So that had been the meaning of Julian's little smile. . . .

The oddest thing of all was that, even as the water rose higher and higher, she couldn't seem to bring herself to believe it.

Julian wanted her *dead?* Oh, it shouldn't be surprising—he was evil, wasn't he? Completely evil. And he'd been in a fury when he left.

But—*dead?*

The water was around her thighs now. It was cold—painfully cold. What a waste it had been to dry her jeans off earlier.

Without consciously knowing how she'd gotten there, she found herself kneeling on one of the waterfall's steps, pressing her hands against the crack, trying to stuff a rock inside. It did no good at all; she could feel the water gushing out in the dark, chilling her hands.

Maybe Julian just wanted to humiliate her—to frighten her until she begged for help. But, no, that didn't make sense. Julian knew she wouldn't beg. She wouldn't give in to him. He'd found that out when he'd set the bees on her in the first Game. Jenny had been willing to die then rather than surrender to him.

And so he must know she would be now, and so he must *want* her dead, really dead.

Unless—

Jenny wouldn't have thought it possible for her to become more frightened than she already was. She'd have thought there would be some limit, that her mind would go numb. But although her body was numbing with cold, her mind was suddenly reeling with a new idea that made sheer black horror sweep through her.

What if Julian didn't know? What if he weren't the one doing this?

Julian had stormed off in a rage—and then *they* had come. What if this water was *their* doing?

She'd be dead before he found out.

The thought resounded in her mind with a queer certainty. Julian had been at odds with the other

Shadow Men once before—when five-year-old Jenny had first opened her grandfather's closet. The other Shadow Men had wanted to kill her, their lawful prey. But Julian had objected. He'd wanted her, wanted her alive.

And she'd stayed alive, because her grandfather had given himself up to them. But now . . .

Now, she thought, they're finishing the job. And Julian *doesn't* know.

It was odd, but she was suddenly sure of that. Julian might be evil, but the other Shadow Men were worse. More twisted, more malign. In the paper house, Julian had controlled everything—but she wasn't in the paper house now. She was in the Shadow World itself, and *all* the Shadow Men were masters.

The water was up to her neck. So cold, Jenny thought—and then the idea came.

What if it got more cold—ice cold? Julian had conjured up a torch with the torch rune, Kenaz. So, maybe—

She was so numb she hardly knew whether she was crawling or floating, but she found the top step and she found the rock she'd tried to stuff in the crack. She was blind, but she could feel the wall, and the rune she wanted was the simplest shape imaginable.

Just one stroke, up and down. A capital *I* without any bars. The ice rune, Isa.

She scratched it directly over the crack, directly in the flow of water. And then, blind and almost paralyzed, she waited.

It was too cold for her to tell at first if it worked.

But then she felt jagged sharpness instead of the smooth numbing gusher.

The flow over the rune Isa had become a frozen waterfall. Although the water around Jenny remained liquid, it had stopped rising.

I did it! I stopped the water! It's ice, beautiful ice!

She sucked in deep breaths of air excitedly, not afraid to use it up any longer. Oh, God, it was good to breathe. And the rune, the rune had worked for her. She couldn't control the Shadow World with her mind, but the runes worked for anyone.

It was only after a few minutes that she realized she was going to die anyway.

Not by drowning—or at least not entirely, although that would come at the end. She was going to freeze to death.

It was too cold—had been too cold even before she had frozen the waterfall. Being here was like floating in the ocean the night the *Titanic* had sunk. She was going to die of hypothermia—lose consciousness and sink. And *then* drown.

And there was nothing at all she could do about it.

She was already too weak when her stupefied mind stumbled upon the idea of the torch rune. Kenaz. If she could remember it—if she could find her rock—or move her fingers . . .

But the rock was gone and her fingers were too anesthetized and her brain was fogging up. Blanking out gently, almost like the beginning of sleep. Kenaz . . . she waved the frozen lumps of flesh that were her hands vaguely under the water, but of course no torch appeared. Water could be frozen into ice, but not kindled into fire. She couldn't change the rules of the elements at her whim.

Disconnected scraps of thought drifted through her mind. It didn't hurt much anymore. Not so bad. And nothing seemed so urgent—whatever had been bothering her moments earlier wasn't as important now.

Help. She had a vague feeling that she might call for help. But it seemed—it seemed there was some reason not to.

Wouldn't hear me. That's it. Was that it? He wouldn't hear me anyway. Too far away.

It didn't matter now. Nothing mattered.

Gebo, she thought, one flash of coherence, of memory, just before her head slid under the water. Gebo, the rune of sacrifice.

7

Oh, Tom.

Dying was painless—but sad. It hurt to think of the people she was leaving behind.

She kept picturing her parents, imagining what they would say when Dee and the others got home and told them. *If* Dee and the others got home and told them.

Her thoughts were very scattered, like dandelion fluff blowing erratically on the wind.

Mr. and Mrs. Parker-Pearson—Summer's parents—had been so hurt when they lost Summer. Jenny hated to think of her parents hurt that way.

And Tom . . . what would happen to Tom? Maybe Julian would let him go. No point in keeping him after Jenny was gone. But that didn't seem likely. Julian was a Shadow Man, he belonged to a race that didn't have gentle emotions. They weren't capable of pity.

Julian might take out his anger on Tom instead.

Please, no, Jenny thought . . . but it didn't seem to matter that much anymore. Even her sadness was fading now—breaking up and floating away. She was dead, and she couldn't change anything.

Strange, though, that a dead person could suddenly feel pain—physical pain. A burning. The frigid water had stopped hurting a long time ago, and since then she'd had no sense of her own body. Trapped in absolute darkness and utter silence, too numb to feel any sensation, she didn't seem to *have* a body. She was just a drifting collection of thoughts.

But now—this burning had started. At first it seemed very distant and easy to ignore. But it didn't stop. It got worse. She felt heat: a tingling, prickling heat that demanded her attention. And with the heat she began to have a body again.

Hands. She could feel her hands now. And feet, she had feet. She had a face, defined by thousands of tiny red-hot needles. And she was aware of a vague, fuzzy glow.

Open your eyes, she told herself.

She couldn't. They were too heavy, and everything hurt so much. She wanted to go back into the darkness where there wasn't any pain. She willed the light to go away.

"Jenny! Jenny!"

Her name, called in tones of love and desperation. Poor Tom, she thought dimly. Tom needed her—and he must be frantic with worry. She should go to Tom.

But it *hurt*.

"Jenny. Please, Jenny, come back—"

Oh, no. No, don't cry. It'll be all right.

There was only one way to make it all right, and that was to come back. Forget how much it hurt.

All right, *do* it, then. Jenny concentrated on the fuzzy glow, trying to make it come closer. Pulling herself toward it. The pain was terrible—her lungs hurt. But if she had lungs, she could breathe. Breathe, girl!

It hurt like hell, and darkness sucked at her, trying to drag her down again.

"That's it, Jenny. Keep fighting! Oh, Jenny . . ."

With a tremendous effort she opened her eyes. Golden light dazzled her. Someone was rubbing her hands.

I did it for you, Tom.

But it wasn't Tom. It was Julian.

Julian was the one rubbing her hands, calling out to her. Golden light danced on his hair, his face. It was a fire, Jenny realized slowly, and she was in another cavern, slightly bigger than the last. She was dry, somehow, and lying in a sort of nest of white fur, very soft, very comfortable. The heat of the fire was bringing her back to life.

The pain wasn't so bad now, although there was still an unyielding knot of ice in her middle. And she felt weak—too weak and exhausted to think properly. It was Julian, not Tom—but she couldn't really take that in.

It didn't even *look* like Julian . . . because Jenny had never seen Julian look afraid. But now the blue eyes were dark with fear and as wide as a child's—the pupils huge and dilated with emotion. Julian's face, which had always seemed molded for arrogance and mockery, was white even in the firelight—and thinner somehow, as if the skin were drawn tight over bones. As for the dangerously beautiful smile that usually curved Julian's lips . . . there wasn't a trace of it.

Strangest of all, Julian seemed to be *shaking.* The hands that held Jenny's had stopped their rubbing, but a fine, continuous tremor ran through them. And Jenny could see how quickly he was breathing by the way his chest rose and fell.

"I thought you were dead," he said in a muted voice.

So did I. Jenny tried to say it, but only got as far as a hitching breath.

"Here. Drink this, it should help." And the next moment he was supporting her head, holding a steaming cup to her lips. The liquid was hot and sweet, and it sent warmth coursing into the cold, hard knot inside her, loosening it and chasing away the last of the pain. Jenny felt herself relaxing, lying still to absorb the fire's heat. A feeling of well-being crept through her as Julian laid her back down.

Gently. Julian was being gentle . . . but Julian was never gentle. He belonged to a race that didn't have gentle emotions. They didn't feel tenderness, weren't capable of pity.

She probably shouldn't even accept help from him—but he looked so haunted, like someone who had been through a terrible fright.

"I thought I'd lost you," he said.

"Then you didn't send the water?"

He just looked at her.

It didn't seem to be the time for recriminations. Oh, she probably *ought* to say something—maybe list the kind of things he'd done to her in the past. He'd hunted her in every way imaginable.

But here, now, in this little cavern surrounded by rock, with no one present but the two of them, and no sound but the soft roar and crackle of the fire . . . all that seemed very far away. Part of a past life. Julian didn't seem like a Shadow Man, didn't seem like a hunter. After all, if he were a predator, he had his quarry right here, exhausted and helpless. He'd never have a better chance. If he wanted her, she wouldn't even be able to put up a fight.

Instead, he was looking at her with those queer dazed eyes, still black with emotion.

"You would have cared if I died," she said slowly.

The eyes searched hers a moment, then looked away.

"You really don't know, do you?" he said in an odd voice.

Jenny said nothing. She pulled herself up a little in the white nest, so she was sitting.

"I've told you how I feel about you."

"Yes. But . . ." Julian had always said that he was in love with her—but Jenny had never sensed much tenderness in the emotion. She might have said this, but for some reason it seemed—inappropriate—to say it to someone who looked so lost. Like a child waiting for a blow. "But I've never understood why."

"Haven't you." It wasn't even a question.

"We're so different." Madness to be talking about

this. But they were both looking at each other, now, quietly, as they had never sat and looked before. Eyes unwavering—but without challenge. It meant something to look into someone's eyes this long, Jenny thought. She shouldn't be doing it.

But of course she had wondered, she had wondered from the beginning what he could possibly see in her. How he could want her—so much. Enough to watch over her since she was five years old, to pierce the veil between the worlds to come after her, to hunt her and stalk her as if he thought about nothing else.

"Why, Julian?" she said softly.

"Would you like a list?" His face was completely blank, his voice clipped and emotionless.

"A—what?"

"Hair like liquid amber, eyes green as the Nile," he said, seeming utterly dispassionate about it. He could have been reading a page of homework assignments. "But it's not the color, really, it's the expression. The way they go so deep and soft when you're thinking."

Jenny opened her mouth, but he was going on.

"Skin that *glows,* especially when you're excited. A golden sheen all over you."

"But—"

"But there are lots of beautiful girls. Of course. You're different. There's something inside you that makes you different, a certain kind of spirit. You're —innocent. Sweet, even after everything that's been thrown at you. Gentle, but with a spirit like flame."

"I'm *not,"* Jenny said, almost frightened. "Audrey sometimes says I'm too simple—"

"Simple as light and air—things people take for granted but that they'd die without. People really should think more about that."

Jenny did feel frightened now. This new Julian was dangerous—made her feel weak and dizzy.

"When I first saw you, you were like a flood of sunshine. All the others wanted to kill you. They thought I was crazy. They laughed. . . ."

He means the other Shadow Men, Jenny thought.

"But I knew, and I watched you. You grew up and got more beautiful. You were so different from anything in my world. The others just watched, but I *wanted* you. Not to kill or to use up the way—the way they do with humans sometimes here. I needed you."

There was something in his voice now besides clinical dispassion. It was—hunger, Jenny thought, but not the cold, malicious hunger she'd seen in the ancient eyes and the whispering voices of the other Shadow Men. It was as if Julian was hungry for something he'd never had, filled with a crippling need even he didn't understand.

"I couldn't *see* anything else, couldn't *hear* anything else. All I could think about was you. I wouldn't let anyone else hurt you, ever. I knew I had to have you, no matter what happened. They said I was crazy with love."

He had gotten up and walked away to the edge of the firelight. As he stood there, Jenny seemed to see him for the first time, looking at him with new eyes. And he looked—small. Small and almost vulnerable.

Nothing in the universe was moving except her heart, and that was shaking her body.

She had never thought about what the other Shadow Men might say to Julian. She knew he was the youngest of a very old race, but she'd never thought about his life at all, or his point of view. She hadn't thought about him *having* a point of view.

"What's it like, being—" She hesitated.

"Being a Shadow Man? Watching from the dark places everything happening on the worlds that aren't full of shadows? Earth has colors, you know, that you never find here."

"But—you can make anything you want. You can create it."

"It's not the same. Things fade here. They don't last."

"But why do you *stay* here, then? Instead of just watching us, you could—" Jenny stopped again. God, what was she saying? Inviting the Shadow Men to her own world? She took a deep breath. "If you could change—"

"I can't change what I am. None of us can. The rest of the nine worlds keep us out; they say our nature is destructive. We're not welcome anywhere—but we'll always be near Earth, watching. From the shadows."

There was something in his voice—too quiet and closed-off for bitterness. A—remoteness that was bleak beyond words.

"Forever," he finished.

"Forever? You never die?"

"Something that isn't born can't die. We have a—beginning, of course. Our names carved on a runestave, a special runestave." He said, almost mockingly, "The stave of life."

There had been something about staves in her grandfather's journal. A picture scrawled in ink, showing a sort of tall, flat branch with runes on it.

"Carve our names on the stave—and we come into existence," Julian said. "Cut them out—and we disappear."

It seemed very heartless to Jenny. Cold—but then the Shadow Men were cold. Not flesh and blood, but creatures that came into being through a carving in wood or stone.

How cold to *be* a Shadow Man, she thought. And how sad. Condemned by your own destructiveness to be what you were forever.

Julian was still standing at the edge of the firelight, face half in shadow, gazing at the darkness beyond. It gave Jenny a queer hollow feeling.

What would it have been like, she wondered suddenly, if he hadn't tried to force her?

From the beginning Julian had used force and trickery. He'd lured her into the More Games store and enticed her into buying the Game, knowing that when she put the paper house together it would suck her into the Shadow World. He'd *kidnapped* her. And then he'd appeared and bullied her: forced her to play his own demonic game to try and win her freedom. He'd threatened her, hurt her friends—*killed* Summer. He'd done everything to try and wring submission out of her.

"Couldn't you just have come and asked?" she murmured.

She'd said the same thing to him in the tower of the paper house. *Didn't that ever occur to you? That you could just appear at my front door, no games, no threats, and just* ask *me?* But in the tower the words had been part of a ruse to get free, and she hadn't really thought about them herself.

Now she did. What if Julian *had* come to her, appearing some night out of the shadows while she was walking home, say, and told her that he loved her? What would she have done?

She would have been afraid. Yes. But after the fear? If Julian had come, offering gifts, gentle, looking as vulnerable as he did now?

If she had accepted his gifts . . .

It was a strange future, too strange to visualize, really, but queerly thrilling. It was too foreign to imagine: herself as a sort of princess with a prince of darkness as consort. For just an instant Jenny got a rushing, heady glimpse; for a fraction of a second she could picture it.

Herself, wearing black silk and sable, sitting on a black marble throne in a big stone hall where it was always twilight. Growing paler and colder, maybe, as she forgot about the ordinary world she'd left behind—but happy, maybe, in her power and position. Would she have little Shadow World creatures to order around and look after? Servants? Would she be able to control the elements here the way Julian did?

Or maybe not a black gown—maybe white, with little icicles all over it, like Hans Christian Andersen's Snow Queen. And jewels like frost-flowers around her neck and a blue-eyed white tiger crouching at her feet. What would Dee and Audrey think if they saw her like that? They might be afraid at first—but she'd serve them strange drinks, like the sweet, hot stuff in the mug, and after a while they'd get used to it. Audrey would envy the pretty things, and Dee would envy the power.

What else? Julian had said she could have anything—*anything.* If she could have anything in the world she wanted, with no limits, no restrictions on her imagination—if she could have *anything* . . .

I'd want Tom.

She'd forgotten him for a moment, because the picture of the big stone hall was so alien. Tom's warmth and strength and lazy smile didn't fit there at all—which of course made sense because Julian would never let him in. But any world without Tom was a world Jenny didn't want.

The vision of the white gown and the jewels disappeared, and she knew somehow that it would never come back, not the way it had for that one moment, when she could feel it and believe in it. She would never forget it, but she would never be able to recapture it, either.

Just as well, she thought unsteadily. She didn't want to think about this anymore; in fact, she thought it was high time that she got out of here. She was tingling all over with a sense of danger.

"I'm warm now," she said, pushing the white fur away. All she could think of was that she had to leave. She should thank him, maybe, for saving her life—

although it wouldn't have been in danger in the first place if not for him.

He was looking at her. Jenny looked away, concentrated on getting her legs under her. When she stood, they were wobbly. She tried to step out of the white nest, and stumbled.

He was there in an instant.

She felt his warm hands close around her arms, steadying her. She stared at his chest, bare under the leather vest and lifting quickly with his breathing. The firelight touched everything with gold.

She didn't want to look up into his face, but somehow it happened anyway.

His eyes were still hugely dilated, the blue mere circles around pupils dark and bottomless as midnight. His pupils always sprang open for her, she realized, but just now there was something haunting about those lonely depths.

"I'm sorry," she whispered, hardly knowing what she meant. "I have to leave now. I'm sorry."

"I know."

In that instant he seemed to understand better than she did herself. He looked very young, and very tired, and heavy with some knowledge she didn't share. Face still solemn, he leaned in slightly.

Jenny shut her eyes.

It was different from any kiss they'd ever had. Not because it was softer—Julian's kisses were usually soft, at the beginning anyway. Not even because it was so slow—Julian's kisses were almost always slow. But it *was* different, in a way that sent Jenny's mind spinning into confusion.

Feeling . . . that was it. Not just sensation, but emotion. Emotion so strong that it left her shaking. It was such an innocent kiss, so—*chaste.* His warm mouth touching hers. His lips trembling against hers. How could something that simple move her so much?

Because she could sense his feelings, she realized. When she touched his lips, she could feel his pain, the almost unendurable pain of someone whose heart was breaking with sadness. What she tasted on those warm, soft lips was unbearable loss. If he'd been dying, or she had, she would have been able to understand such a kiss.

He's suffering like that—from losing *me?* Jenny had never been particularly modest, but she could hardly believe it. She might have rejected the idea outright—except for what she was feeling herself.

What she felt . . . was a shattering inside.

When he stepped back, Jenny was in something like a trance. She stood there, eyes shut, still *feeling* everything, unable to move. Tears welled up around her lashes.

But Tom.

The time in sixth grade when he'd broken his leg and sat in a tide pool, white but still wisecracking, holding on to Jenny's hand, not letting anybody else see how bad the pain was. All the many times he'd held Jenny for *her* sake, when she got scared at movies, or when she cried over the stray animals she took in. He'd stayed up all night when she thought Cosette, the kitten she'd rescued from a vacant lot, was dying. He had been part of her life since she was seven years old. He was a part of *her.*

And Julian had hurt him. Julian had blown his chance right at the very beginning, when he'd done that.

Jenny opened her eyes, the trance broken. She stepped back, and saw Julian's face change. As if he knew exactly what she was thinking.

"Tom needs me," she said.

Julian smiled then, grimly, in a way that chased the cobwebs out of Jenny's brain. The lost, haunted look was gone, as if it had never existed.

"Oh, yes. Tommy needs you like air. But I need you like—"

"What?" Jenny said when it was clear he wasn't going on.

"Like light," Julian said, with the same bitter smile. "You're light, all right—like a flame to a moth. I told you once that you shouldn't mess with forbidden things—I should have taken my own advice."

"Light shouldn't be *forbidden,"* Jenny said.

"It is to me. It's deadly to a Shadow Man. Light kills shadows, don't you know? And of course the other way around."

He seemed to find this amusing. He'd done one of his quicksilver mood changes, and looking at his face now, Jenny almost wondered if the last half hour had been a dream.

"Don't think that just because I pulled you out of the water, the Game is over," he added. "You need three gold coins to get to your precious Tommy. And time's *tick, tick, ticking. . . .*"

"I've got one, remember. I—" Jenny broke off with an inarticulate noise, feeling in her jeans pocket. The Swiss Army knife was still there, but the gold doubloon he'd tossed her in the cavern was gone.

"But I *had* it. It must have fallen out—"

"Sorry. Only one turn to a customer. No replays. Do not pass Go, do not collect two hundred dollars."

"You—" Jenny broke off again. Her anger drained, but she felt something inside herself harden, ice over. All right, then. She must have been crazy, feeling sorry for Julian—*Julian!*—but now she knew better. They were opponents, as always, playing against each other in a Game that was as cutthroat and pitiless as Julian himself.

"I'll get the coins—if you give me the chance. I can't do much in here," she said.

"True. Exit doors are to the left. Please watch your step and keep moving. We hope you've enjoyed the ride."

Jenny turned and saw a rectangle of dim light. It hadn't been there before.

She took a breath and started toward it, careful to walk straight.

She didn't mean to look back. But as she got close to the door, close enough to see that it looked like an ordinary double door, like the kind that led out of Space Mountain at Disneyland, she threw a quick glance over her shoulder.

He was standing where she'd left him, a black

silhouette in front of the fire. She couldn't tell anything by his posture.

She turned away and stepped through the door, blinking. She could see tiny distant lights, lots of them, sparkling and wheeling in a dazzling display.

"What—?" she whispered.

Something grabbed her.

8

Thank *God!"* a voice shouted in Jenny's ear. Jenny relaxed against the slim but very strong arms holding her.

"Dee—you scared me to death. . . ." The lights were on the canopy of the merry-go-round across the lake. It was turning and Jenny could hear faint music from a Wurlitzer band organ.

"You scared *us* to death," Audrey said. "Where have you been for the last two hours? We ran down that shaft with the roof caving in right behind us all the way—and then when we finally got to the mouth of the cave, we realized you weren't with us. Then Dee went crazy and tried to go back while everything was still falling, but it almost killed us and we had to go out—and when we *got* out, it was just a ride again."

"The caving-in noise stopped," Michael explained, "and I looked back and the cave was fiberglass again."

"And empty," Dee said, giving Jenny a fierce hug before letting go. "We walked all through it, the three of us, and you weren't in it. It was just a mine ride."

"That is the Emergency Exit we just came out of," Audrey said, pointing a finger at Jenny's door. "So the question is, where have you been? You've seen him, haven't you?"

Jenny was looking down at herself by the light of a nearby fountain—a fountain which had been dark when they'd first gone into the ride. Her jeans were rumpled but dry, her hair was all ridges and waves, the way it got when it dried without her brushing it. The supplies she'd packed so carefully to help her face the Shadow World were gone. Even her flashlight was gone.

"I saw him," she told Audrey briefly without looking at her. "I found out what the new Game is." She explained what Julian had told her about finding the three doubloons to get to Zach and Tom. She didn't say anything about the other Shadow Men, or the rising water in the dark cave, or how it had felt to die. She wanted to; she wanted to talk about it in privacy, and maybe cry, and be comforted, safe with her friends. But she *wasn't* safe, and there wasn't any privacy, and what was the point of alarming everybody?

As for Julian and his bizarre mood swings—she didn't even want to get on the subject.

"So at least we got something out of that ride," Michael said. "I mean, it nearly killed us, and we lost most of our stuff, but we did get some weapons, and now we know what we're doing. What happens after we collect these doubloons?"

"I think we go to the bridge, just like that kid said in the regular park," Jenny said. She was grateful—and proud. They were all battered and tired, and there were only two flashlights left—but no one was even talking about giving up.

"The bridge must be on the other side of the lake, around back," she added. "When we get there, I guess Julian will let us across." She looked at the lake. The merry-go-round lights were reflected in it, and so were other lights, blue and green and gold, from the island itself. Shadows of trees broke them up.

In the center of the island, standing very tall and white, was the lighthouse. It looked the same as the one Jenny had seen that afternoon, in the real park, except that now it was illuminated like the Washington Monument. Like a tower for imprisoned princes.

"That's where Tom and Zach are," she said quietly.

"Where should we start looking?" Dee said, equally quiet.

The Emergency Exit door had brought Jenny out close to the front of the mine ride. "Well—we could go left to Kiddieland," she said, "or right, back the way we came from the Fish Pond. Or around the front of the lake, toward the merry-go-round."

Michael ran a hand through his rumpled dark hair. "Let's go around the lake—it'll take us by the billboard about the contest. Maybe that'll give us a clue."

"That's where we came in tonight," Audrey said. "When we came through the door with the runes, I mean."

They walked past the dark ringtoss booth and around the gentle northern curve of the lake. There seemed to be no rhyme or reason as to which parts of the park were awake and which still slept.

They kept a close eye out for things like the one that had attacked Dee, but they saw nothing. Then, as they got closer to the billboard, Jenny heard a voice.

A low voice. It scared her—who else was in the park with them?

She rounded a clump of spruce trees and saw a car from a circus train, with a red roof and silver bars.

"I'm Leo the Paper-Eating Lion," the muzzle thrust between the bars said.

Only the voice—was wrong. It wasn't the peppy, friendly tenor of the Leo in the regular park. It had dropped two octaves and become distorted and almost machinelike. A thick, muddy cybervoice.

"Geez," Michael whispered.

Jenny moved cautiously closer, following Dee. The circus car was lighted, very bright and gay against a dark background of bushes. The animal *looked* like the Leo of the ordinary park, with a shiny caramel-colored face, dark mane, and painted body. Jenny's eyes were drawn to the muzzle, spread in a permanent smiling *O* so it could suck up trash. It looked as if it were calling "Yoohoo!"

"I eat all kinds of things," the growling, guttural voice said.

"I bet," breathed Michael.

"What's it doing here? Is it just to scare us?" Audrey said, circling the cart at a safe distance. Dee was playing her flashlight into the plastic muzzle.

"I think there's something in there," she said.

"You're kidding. You *are* kidding, aren't you?" Jenny edged along beside Audrey. She didn't want to get any closer to the lion than she had to—the asphalt path wasn't nearly wide enough in her opinion.

Dee knelt and squinted. "Something gold," she said. "No, really, I'm serious. Look way back in there, in the throat."

Unhappily Jenny took the flashlight and aimed it at the dark hole. It did look as if there might be something shining inside, but gold or silver, she couldn't tell.

"It might just be a gum wrapper," she said.

Dee leaned a casual arm on her shoulder. "Don't tell me, you've had Leo the Lion nightmares."

Jenny hadn't, that she could remember. But the lion had looked sinister even this afternoon, and it looked doubly sinister now.

"I am not putting my hand in there," Michael said positively.

Dee flashed her most barbaric smile. "No, Audrey can do it; she's got nice long nails. How about it, Aud?"

"Don't tease her," Jenny said absently. "Now, what we need is something long—but a fishing pole wouldn't work because it wouldn't catch a coin. Maybe if we put something sticky on the end . . ."

"Nothing's as good as a hand. Audrey could—"

"Dee, quit it!" Jenny cast a sharp look at the girl beside her. She didn't know why Dee and Audrey seemed to be having problems today—maybe it was a reaction to all the tension—but this was no time for Dee's skewed sense of humor. Audrey was standing a little apart from the others, head tilted back, chestnut eyes narrowed in disdain, cherry-colored lips pursed. She looked very cool and superior.

"Leo's *always* hungry. So feed me," the distorted, bestial voice said. Every time it spoke, Jenny's heart jumped. She was terrified that the caramel-colored muzzle might *move,* that she'd look up and Leo's head would swing toward her.

It can't. It's plastic, she thought. But she was afraid her heart would simply stop if it did. The quietness of the park around them, the darkness, made this one animated trash can even more eerie.

Dee sat back on her heels. "It looks like there's more to this than just finding the coins. We have to actually *get* them, which may be the hardest part. It's a quest game."

"Quest?" Jenny said.

"Yeah. Remember how I told you about the different kinds of games, once? Games fall into certain categories. The first one Julian played with us, where we had to get to the top of the house by dawn, that was a race game."

"Right, and the second one, where the animals were chasing us, was a hunting game. Like hide-and-seek," Jenny said.

"Yeah, well, there's another type of game, where you have to find things in order to win—like in a treasure hunt or a scavenger hunt. Or hot and cold. A quest game. It's as old as the other kinds of games."

"Naturally," Michael said. "Humans are terrific questers—they love to look for things. The Holy

Grail, or the truth, or the treasures in Zork, or whatever."

"Surely you can find something to feed Leo the Paper-Eating Lion. I'm *starving.*"

Jenny looked up, jerked out of the pleasant hypothetical discussion. Audrey was standing by the circus car, examining her nails. The usually perfect polish had been slightly chipped in the mine ride. She looked thoughtful.

"Go on, princess. I dare you," Dee said, her black eyes flashing in amusement.

"Don't be silly, Audrey," Jenny said automatically. The concept was so ridiculous, though, that she said it unhurriedly. Audrey never did anything reckless—not physically reckless, at least.

So Jenny didn't say the warning with urgency, and therefore she was, in some way, responsible for what happened next.

Audrey put her hand in.

Michael was the one who shouted. Jenny jumped up. But for a moment it looked as if it was going to be all right.

Audrey, her face set, was fishing around in the hole. Her hand was in it to the wrist.

"I feel something," she said.

Jenny's heart was thudding. "Oh, Audrey . . ."

Audrey's lips curved in a triumphant smile that brought out her beauty mark. "It's cold—I've got it!"

Then everything happened very fast.

The caramel-colored plastic face was flowing, melting, like a very good morphing effect in a movie.

In a movie it would have been fascinating—but here it was real. It was *real,* and so awful that it froze Jenny to the spot.

The colors bled and changed, going olive green, then a dreadful grayish cemetery tone with steely streaks. The eyes sank, becoming hollow pits. The mouth seemed to snarl, lips pulling back to reveal long teeth that had grown to trap Audrey's wrist.

It happened so fast that even Dee didn't have time to move. Audrey started to gasp, and then screamed instead. Her entire body snapped forward.

The thing had sucked her arm in to the elbow.

"Audrey!" Michael shouted. He covered the distance to her in two steps. Dee was right behind him with her pick.

No good, Jenny thought dazedly. It's not flesh, like that thing—like Slug. It's stone or metal or something.

"Don't hit it, Dee. That won't help—that won't help. We have to pull her out!"

The thing—it wasn't a lion anymore, but some sort of hideous cyberbeast—was now the color of an old statue coated with moss.

Audrey screamed again, breathlessly, and her body jerked. The nylon jacket was skinned up to her shoulder now, bunched like an inner tube as her arm was dragged farther in.

"It's taking my arm off!"

Jenny gasped, almost sobbing. Michael was yanking at Audrey.

"No, don't pull! Don't pull! It hurts!"

Vaseline, Jenny was thinking. Or soap—something to make it slippery. But they didn't have anything.

"Dee!" she said. "Use the pick—try to pry its teeth apart. Michael, wait until she gets it in—*then* pull."

Audrey was still screaming and Michael was crying. Vaguely, in shock, Jenny noticed that the stone beast was still changing, becoming more deformed. Dee wedged the tip of the heavy pick upside down between the gray, mossy teeth and pulled back on the handle. Jenny grabbed it to help her.

"Hard!"

Dee threw her weight down. Jenny prayed the wooden handle wouldn't break off from the iron head.

She felt something shift—the upper jaw lifting just a fraction, like a car lifting on a jack.

"Pull, Michael!"

Michael pulled. Audrey's arm came out.

She screamed on a new note—a shriek that pierced Jenny's chest. But her arm came out.

They all fell backward, the pick clattering down. With a common impulse they scrabbled back away from the circus car, still sitting, still holding on to one another.

It was only then that Jenny looked at Audrey's arm.

There were toothmarks. Or—some kind of marks, as if sharp rocks had been scraped over the skin. Long, raw gouges, just starting to bleed.

"Audrey—oh, God, are you okay?" Michael was gasping.

A gurgling, maniacal voice said, "I bet I'll have a tummyache tomorrow."

Jenny looked. The cyber-beast had stopped changing, its features frozen in a long-toothed snarl.

Dee raised a clenched fist, tendons cording in her slender arm. Then she dropped it. "I don't think it can move toward us," she said in a curiously quenched voice. Jenny glanced at her, but Dee turned and Jenny found herself looking at the back of her close-cropped head, where velvety nubs of hair glistened like mica.

"Does anybody have aspirin?" Jenny said. "I lost mine."

Michael, who had taken off his sweatshirt and was trying to wrap Audrey's arm in his undershirt, thrust a hand in his pocket. "I've got some . . . here."

Audrey's left hand was trembling as she took them, washing them down with a gulp of water from the canteen Dee silently offered.

"*Are* you okay?" Jenny asked hesitantly.

Audrey took another drink of water. Her spiky lashes were dark against her cheek as she leaned back against Michael. She looked as white as porcelain, and as fragile. But she nodded.

"Really? You can move your arm and everything?" Michael's cotton undershirt was showing signs of pink, but it wasn't the cuts that worried Jenny. She was afraid Audrey's shoulder might be dislocated.

Audrey nodded again. A faint smile appeared on her lips. She lifted her right arm, the bandaged one, and turned it over. Then, slowly, she unclenched her fist.

On her palm, gold as a buttercup, was a coin.

Michael gave a shout of laughter.

"You got it! You wouldn't let go, you little—" He seized Audrey in a bear hug.

"You may kiss me," Audrey said. "Just don't squish my arm." She twisted her head toward Dee. "Good thing your pick wasn't flimsy. No rawhide there!"

It was an extraordinarily generous gesture, but Dee seemed to take it as an insult. At least, when Jenny looked at Dee, she could only see the fine curve of a dark cheekbone.

"If everybody can move, we'd better go," Dee said. "We're right in the open here; anything could be sneaking up on us."

Jenny helped Audrey up as Michael put his sweatshirt back on. The lion-thing in the painted cage watched them like a gargoyle.

"What should we do with the coin?" Audrey said.

"I'll take it." Jenny put this one in the pocket of her pale blue denim shirt and buttoned the pocket. "If we can get to the merry-go-round, we can rest. There's an arbor thing beside it."

The merry-go-round had gone dark, but across the shimmering water of the lake Jenny could see the shining lighthouse. Tom was there—and Zach. Jenny had to get to them, no matter what happened on the way.

Audrey didn't want to rest long. "If I don't get up now, I never will. But where do we go?"

"That lion was lit-up—working," Michael said. "And it had a doubloon."

"So we just look for something else that's working?"

"I don't like the idea of being led," Dee said, but she said it without her usual confidence.

Jenny was worried about Dee. Of course she hadn't meant for anybody to get hurt. She'd just been trying to get a rise out of Audrey. But the way it had turned out—

"What are those lights way down there?" Michael said.

Beyond the merry-go-round, beyond a stretch of greenery, tiny white lights twinkled between dark trees.

"I think—I think it may be the arcade," Jenny said.

"Well, it's working," said Michael.

"Allons-y," Audrey said, settling things.

They passed the dark merry-go-round and a rocket ride with all the rockets landed, down. As they rounded a slight turn in the path, a building came into view.

Hundreds of tiny white lights flashed, running along the borders of a sign reading: PENNY ARCADE. Jenny stopped in her tracks.

"But—it's different. It's not like it was this afternoon. It's like—" Suddenly she knew. "It's like it *used* to be. This is the way the arcade looked when I was a kid. I remember!"

"Well, it's open," Michael said.

The doors gaped invitingly. Jenny felt a qualm as they cautiously stepped over the threshold. She didn't know why Julian had made the arcade this way, but she couldn't imagine it meant anything good.

Still, it gave her a strange pang of pleasure to see what was inside the building. Not the gleaming, spotless, high-tech wonderland she'd seen in the real park that day. Now it was a dim, rather dingy room, crowded with old-fashioned wooden cabinets.

Automata, Jenny remembered. That's what her grandfather had called the machines with moving figures inside them. She remembered him taking her here, putting dimes in the slots, watching the mechanical action scenes.

Her grandfather had always seemed to have time for her. All she knew as a kid was that he was a professor of this, that, and the other, but he never seemed to go to work anywhere. He was always home when Jenny and Zach came to visit—unless he was traveling. He did a lot of traveling, and always brought back presents.

"What was that? There—at the back," Michael said.

Jenny looked, but only saw more cabinets.

"It's gone now. I thought it was one of those little critters—the scuttling ones." He spotted something. "Hey, you want some candy peanuts? I found lots of change in with the aspirin."

The machine dispensed black candy-coated peanuts, very stale, and square multicolored gum. Jenny felt a little better while chewing it, comforted somehow.

And the machines were interesting, in the absurd, picturesque way of times gone by. There were peep shows and nickelodeons and all sorts of mechanized figures.

"The Ole Barn Dance," Jenny read on one cabinet. "See 'em Whoop It Up! Watch 'em Swing! Drop two bits in the box."

The little figures were made of blocks of wood, dangling from wires. Their wooden jaws hung open grotesquely.

"Do you think we should try the things?" Audrey said doubtfully. Jenny knew what she meant—after what had happened with Leo, she didn't relish the thought of activating anything mechanical.

"I guess we have to," she said slowly. "In case the coin's inside one of them. Just stay back from them—and if anything goes on by itself, run."

"And check the coin slots," Audrey said sensibly. "What better place to hide a doubloon?"

They moved carefully around the dim room, staying together, checking the tops and bottoms of cabinets for a gleam of gold.

Michael found a mutoscope and began cranking it, leaning gingerly to look in the goggle-type viewer and watch the flip-card film. SEE NAUGHTY MARIETTA SUN BATHING, the sign on the brass-trimmed machine read. PASSED BY NY CENSORS, OCT. 12, 1897.

"M'arm hurts," he said afterward. "And it's just some lady wrapped in a sheet."

Audrey paused in front of an elaborately carved machine with gold paint that was much faded and rubbed off. Dee found a cabinet that looked like a grandfather clock, labeled: SEE HORRIBLE MONSTER. TERRIFYING—SHOCKING—ONLY 5 CENTS. Jenny knew that machine: You put your money in and saw a mirror.

Jenny ventured a little farther down the corridor.

Not that grip tester—she didn't want to touch it. She didn't want to step on the foot vitalizer, either.

There—a rather shabby wood box with dark glass. The sign read: ASK THE WIZARD. DEPOSIT 10¢ IN SLOT AND THE WIZARD WILL PERFORM FOR YOU. Below was a strip of plastic tape: RECEIVE PREDICTION HERE.

Jenny had always liked the kind of fortune-teller that gave you a card. She loved the outrageous predictions about whether you were going to get married and what your career would be. She picked out a dime.

The coin slot was shaped like a sphinx. Jenny hesitated an instant with the dime resting against cool metal. A flash of foreboding went through her, as if telling her to stop and think before she did anything rash.

But what was rash about turning on a mechanized wizard? And they *had* to search this place.

She slipped the dime in.

9

As the coin clunked somewhere in the machine's innards, Jenny heard a faint buzzing, then a mechanical ticking. The glass brightened, and Jenny could see that two bare lightbulbs had gone on inside.

They illuminated a wizard, maybe two feet high and wearing a surprisingly mournful and pained expression. As Jenny watched, it began to move jerkily, like clockwork.

Its eyes opened and shut, and its eyebrows lifted and fell. Its lower lip seemed to be jointed and moved below a surprisingly fine and lifelike beard, as if it were mumbling to itself. Its face was ruddy plastic, with carmine lips and deep shadows under the eyes. Jenny could see layers of caked-up paint on the cheeks.

Poor thing, she thought. Absurd as it was, she felt sorry for the mechanical figure. It showed much finer workmanship than the barn dancers, but it was undeniably in a state of disrepair. Its paintbrush eyelashes were matted, its black velveteen robe dusted with red lint.

A strange feeling was coming over Jenny. A squeezing in her chest. It was ridiculous to feel this way about an automaton. But it looked so pathetic—so *trapped* there in that box, in front of a stapled-on backdrop of shabby red velveteen. . . .

And something about the figure . . . something about its face . . .

The wizard held a chipped and peeling wand in one clenched fist. He raised the wand and struck it on the table in front of him—Jenny could see the indentation where he'd done it many times before.

His eyes opened and shut, rolled around, moving back and forth. They didn't look at the wand.

His lower lip moved, showing white painted teeth, but there was no sound. He seemed to be talking to himself.

Jenny was mesmerized by the wizard's jerky, almost violent movements—but she didn't know why, and she was getting more and more frightened. It's because he looks like one of those homeless guys at the shelter, she told herself. That's why he's familiar.

No. It was more than that. Something about the plastic face, a face frozen in an expression of ineffable sadness.

The glass eyes rolled, staring straight out at Jenny. Dark as marbles, strangely tired, strangely kind.

She knew.

She really did know then, but it was such an impossible, intolerable concept that she pushed it away. Slam-dunked it back into her subconscious. Too insane to even think about.

She heard a click at the bottom of the machine and saw that a card had appeared. She reached for it reflexively—then stopped for just an instant, again feeling as if her mind was shouting a warning.

Her fingers closed on the card. She turned it over and stared at the writing on the other side.

Then she felt herself begin to faint.

The cramped lines of type were faded but perfectly readable. Not a prediction or a personality chart.

The entire card was covered with two words typed over and over.

HELP ME HELP ME HELP ME HELP ME HELP ME HELP ME HELP ME HELP ME HELP ME HELP ME HELP ME HELP ME HELP ME HELP ME HELP ME . . .

The letters swam in front of Jenny's eyes, merging into a scintillating black-and-white pattern. She couldn't control her trembling or the shuddering in her stomach. She couldn't feel her legs. And she couldn't scream—even though there was a screaming inside her.

She felt the floor bang her palms and rump as her legs gave way.

"What happened? Did it do something to you?" The others were around her. Jenny could only look up at the glass box, the card creasing as her fingers tightened on it.

Those tired dark eyes, oh, yes, they were familiar. But they didn't belong with a shabby velveteen robe and a long angel-hair beard. They belonged with a slight, stooped body, a cardigan sweater, and thinning white hair. And a smell of peppermint, because that was what he always carried in his pockets.

"It's my grandfather," Jenny whispered. "Oh, Dee, it's my *grandfather,* it's my *grandfather. . . ."*

Dee cut a glance at the box. When she looked back at Jenny, her face was composed. "Okay, now, you take it easy. Let's get you some water here."

"No!" Jenny screamed. She was completely out of control. She hit Dee, beating at her feebly with her fists. "Don't *humor* me! It's my grandfather in there —they've done it to him. Oh, God!" Tears were flying as she whipped her head. "It's a joke, don't you see? He was a sorcerer—now he's a wizard. I thought he was dead—but this is so much worse—"

Dee simply grabbed the flailing hands so Jenny couldn't do any harm. Jenny could see Michael's brown eyes, and Audrey's chestnut-colored ones, looking over Dee's shoulder.

"It's true," she gasped, quieting. "Look at the card. He wants help. *He wants out!"*

Michael picked up the card silently, showed it to Dee and Audrey. They all looked at the box.

The wizard was still moving, staring straight ahead with his tragic expression, hitting the table with his wand. His hands were all in one piece, Jenny noticed with wild precision. She could see beads of paint in the slight grooves between the fingers.

She'd thought the Shadow Men would eat him. That was what the hungry eyes in the closet had wanted.

But whatever they'd done with his body, his soul was here.

They'd put it in this—thing. Stuck it in a plastic body, so that he could stand forever, moving like clockwork when the machine was activated, endlessly banging his wand.

Julian had said the Shadow Park had been created ten years ago, and for a special reason. It was ten years ago that her grandfather had disappeared.

"They did it to punish him," she whispered. "They put him here so he could never die—they trapped him the way he trapped them in the closet. . . ." Her voice was rising.

Michael swallowed, looking sick. Dee's nostrils flared.

There was a click and another card appeared in the slot.

Dee reached for it, letting go of Jenny's hands. Jenny scrambled to her knees to see it over Dee's arm.

LOOK IN THE BLACK CABINET.

"There," Michael said. Jenny twisted. Behind her was a shiny black machine with a wide, darkened oval window. It looked relatively new, and a plaque read: SPEAK TO THE SPIRITS. ASK ANY YES OR NO QUESTION, 10¢.

Jenny knew the type of game. The window lit up and a skull nodded or shook its head to answer you.

A wave of icy cold swept over her, as cold as the water in the mine ride.

"Do it, Michael," she whispered and held her breath.

Michael wiped his mouth with the back of his hand. He glanced uncertainly at Jenny, then put a coin in.

The glass brightened. There wasn't a skull inside—there were two heads with closed eyes. They were illuminated from below with a ghastly blue light which clearly showed there was nothing below either neck. At the sight of them, Audrey screamed thinly and Michael retched. Dee grabbed hold of Jenny hard enough to hurt.

"Now do you believe me?" Jenny said, her voice rising again. "They're here, they're all here!"

Michael was pressing his hand to his mouth. Dee was holding on to Jenny. Audrey was still making a thin wheezing noise.

Nobody answered Jenny, but in the cabinet the heads of Slug and P.C. bobbed.

The blue light shone on their chapped, loose-hanging lips. They looked unconscious—as if unseen hands were wagging them by the hair, making them nod.

You guys were so tough, Jenny thought, unable to look away from the cadaverous faces. *Such bad boys. Breaking into my house, stealing the Game. Barging into the Shadow World uninvited. Now you're both here and you don't look so tough. And—*

"Summer," Jenny whimpered. "If Summer—if Summer—"

"Jenny—"

"If we find Summer like *that—"*

There was a click. Dee snatched the card before Jenny could get to it. She read it, holding Jenny away.

"What does it say?"

Slowly Dee turned the card.

LOOK IN THE FUN HOUSE.

"At least it's not another cabinet," Dee said.

Michael said, "You mean, you think it's about Summer?"

"I—maybe. Or"—Dee's face relaxed—"it could be a clue for a doubloon."

Audrey shielded her eyes. "I can't stand those things—make them *stop,*" she said in a ragged voice.

The heads were bobbing slowly up and down, nodding again.

"I think that's our answer," Michael said.

"Yeah, but which is it—Summer or a doubloon?"

"I don't care, I just want to get out of here," Audrey said.

"We can't *go,*" Jenny said to Dee. "We can't leave him, we can't go anywhere." She pulled herself up using the wizard's cabinet as a support, and leaned a hand on it, looking into the glass. "I have to help him."

"Jenny." Dee touched her elbow gently. "There's nothing you can do for him." Then, as Jenny held on to the glass: "All right, what *are* you going to do for him?"

Jenny didn't know. Stay here with him—if she could keep from screaming. Break the cabinet to pieces.

But then what? Could she stand to hold the thing that was in there, cuddle it like a stiff, oversize doll? If she broke the doll, would it kill her grandfather? Or would he still be alive inside his pieces?

He'd rather be dead than be like this, she knew. But how did you kill something that wasn't alive, only trapped?

"Oh, I'm so sorry," she whispered, pressing her hand to the glass. "I'm so sorry, I'm so sorry. . . ."

It was her fault—he'd gone in her place. Given himself to the Shadow Men for her.

But Dee was right. Jenny couldn't do anything for him now.

Her hands trailed down the glass. "We'll go to the fun house."

On their way out she turned back to face the wizard's cabinet, looked into the dark, staring eyes. "I'm coming back," she said. "And when I do, I'll help you."

The heads were bobbing in their case as she left.

Out into the night again. Jenny wished she had a map. Her memory for some parts of the park was sketchy.

"The fun house is up near the very front," she said, "so it's got to be somewhere that way." She pointed the way they'd come.

"Yeah, but more to the left. We can cut across there." Dee was more talkative than she had been since Audrey's accident, but her voice was still not quite itself.

They passed rest rooms, trees, a large refreshment stand. The Tilt-a-Whirl was dark; so was the Enterprise. And so, as they approached it, was the fun house.

Then an uncanny sound began. Two slow, rising notes, repeated over and over. Jenny recognized it.

"The foghorn on the ark."

Lights were going on in the large boat, first outlining the roof, then illuminating the windows of the house on deck. Jenny could see animals in the windows: an elephant, an ostrich, a hippopotamus, and at the very top Father Noah, with an expression more like a leer than a grin.

The ark began to rock visibly.

"Looks like they've got the welcome mat out," Michael said.

They entered through the whale's mouth, walking on the spongy pink tongue. Inside, the doors were slanted, exacerbating the rocking feeling. Jenny began to feel giddy immediately.

She couldn't see much inside. Black lights made Audrey's white nylon jacket glow and Dee's eyes flash. We should have looked for controls, Jenny thought. There must be some way to turn on the lights in these places.

But when she looked back, the door she'd just come through was gone. Instead, there was a glass booth, with a human figure silhouetted inside.

Summer! Jenny's heart gave a terrible jolt. She took a step toward the booth, then stopped. She couldn't tell anything about the figure. She took another step, one hand out toward the glass.

Oh, God, I don't want to see this. . . .

A light in the booth went on.

Wild laughter assaulted Jenny's ears. It was the sound of somebody going insane, and at first it frightened her so much that she couldn't take in what she was seeing.

Then she focused on the figure. It was a hugely fat woman, bucktoothed, with freckles like birthmarks and scraggly hair. Her hands waved in front of her as she cackled and guffawed.

I remember that! Laughing—oh, *what* was her name? Laughing Lizzie. She used to be in the arcade, and she always scared me.

Jenny scanned the florid face, looking for something familiar in the empty eyes.

Could Summer—be in there?

Summer had been tiny, dimpled, with thistledown blond hair and dark blue eyes. She'd been as light as a flower petal stirred by the wind. Could *they* have destroyed her body and put her in this bloated plastic thing?

Or maybe she was like P.C. and Slug. Maybe there was a table somewhere in here with a piece of Summer's old body on it.

But Jenny couldn't see anything she recognized in the fat woman's eyes. Nothing to make her want to look any closer, especially since the demented laughter was going on and on.

She glanced at the others. "Let's keep moving."

They stumbled through twisted corridors and across shifting floors. A blue Day-Glo hippo gaped at Jenny, a snake dropped from the ceiling in front of her. From all around came panting, growling, weird music—a cacophony of strange sounds. It made it hard for Jenny to hear even Dee and the others right next to her.

And it was hard to examine the exhibits. Chain-link fencing was strung in front of many of them and had to be pulled away. Every figure that looked even vaguely human had to be studied, and anything that looked like gold had to be scrutinized.

"*Everything* in here looks suspicious," Michael said as they stared at a laughing man with three faces that rotated slowly on his neck.

Jenny was most disconcerted by the mirrors. On the floor they mimicked endless drops, reflecting lights down into infinity. On the walls they confused her, duplicating her own wide green eyes, Audrey's copper hair, Michael's pale, set face. It reflected Dee's supple movements, making it seem as if there were dozens of camouflage jackets all going in different directions.

Zach always hated these mirrors, too, Jenny remembered, turning a sharp zigzag corner. Enough that Julian put them in the paper house as part of his nightmare. She suddenly realized that she hadn't thought about her cousin in quite a while. She'd been too busy worrying over Tom—and over how to survive.

But she *did* miss Zach. She missed his winter-gray eyes, and his sharp-featured face, and his dry intelligence. Even if Tom had been safe, she would have come to the Shadow World questing for Zach.

"Ugh," Dee said. "What's *this?*"

They had come out of the mirror maze and were now in dark, windy corridors with very unsteady floorboards. There were displays every few feet—much like museum displays, except that Jenny had never seen this kind of thing in any museum.

"Disgusting," Michael said under his breath. "Replogle, disgusting . . ." Replogle was really the name of a map company, but Michael thought it made a much better adjective.

He was trying to cheer himself up. Because, Jenny thought, the displays really were gruesome. They were torture scenes.

Wax figures were set up as victims and torturers. Some of the equipment Jenny recognized. The rack. The Iron Maiden. The stocks.

And some of it was dreadfully and harrowingly unfamiliar. Boots with handles like the vise Tom's father had in his garage workshop. To break bones, Jenny supposed. Grotesque metal helmets with iron tongues that gagged the victim. Cages too small to stand or lie down in. Every kind of device to burn, or cut, or maim.

"This was *not* here this afternoon," Audrey said.

"It's my fault, I guess," Dee said after a moment. "I went up to San Francisco once with my mom, and there was a place at Fisherman's Wharf—like a chamber of horrors, you know? It gave me nightmares for *years.*"

Abruptly she turned away from the nearest scene and leaned against the wall, head down. She was breathing hard.

Jenny peered through the darkness. "Dee?"

"Yeah. Just give me a minute."

"What are you *mumbling?*"

"It's—it's, uh, this thing for when you get upset. I got it out of—" She paused. "Ancient Chinese manuscripts."

"In what dialect?" Audrey demanded. "Mandarin? Cantonese?"

"All right, it was from a kung fu movie. But it works. It's pretty long, but the end goes 'I am as strong as I need to be. I am my only master.'"

"I am my only master," Jenny repeated. She liked that. Julian and his people might be the masters of this world, but not of *her.* No one was her master if she wouldn't let them be. "Is it helping?" she asked Dee.

"Enough. I don't think I'm going to faint or puke right this moment."

Shock tingled in Jenny's palms. The very idea of

Dee fainting was so outrageous—so frightening—she couldn't cope with it. Dee was *never* that scared.

Only maybe she was, especially when confronted with things that physical courage couldn't do anything about. The stuff around them here was history—and who could change that?

"I'm gonna join Amnesty International if I ever get out of here," Dee muttered. "I swear, I swear."

"Mother and I already belong," Audrey said.

Mrs. Myers? thought Jenny, and Dee said, "Your *mom?"* Audrey's mother was a society matron, good at making finger sandwiches and arranging charity fashion shows. She and Dee didn't get along.

"Maybe all that organization is good for something after all," Dee murmured.

Jenny still had a very bad feeling about the place. She wanted to hurry through it, to not see as much as possible.

And they couldn't. They had to check every figure, staring into faces the color of peach crayons, with teeth that were a little *too* shiny in the spotlights. The skin of the wax figures had an unreal inner glow, as if the outer layers were translucent and the color buried somewhere inside.

But none of the glassy eyes looked like Summer's. And nothing moved, although Jenny was in constant dread that an eyelid would flicker or a chest would rise.

If they start coming to life, I'll go crazy, she thought almost with detachment. Just screaming, staring crazy. It would be a relief to go crazy at this point.

"Jenny—" Michael's voice was choked.

Jenny turned.

"Blue," Michael said, and Jenny saw what he meant.

It was on a table. Above it, suspended by a rusty chain, was a huge wooden disk with bloody iron spikes. It was a little pool of china blue precisely the color of Summer's shirtdress.

Something was inside the dress.

Funny that Jenny could remember that outfit so exactly. Summer had appeared on the doorstep wearing it the night of Tom's birthday party, looking fresh, sweet, and completely inappropriate, since it was freezing outside.

Now it was lying on a table, encasing a body. Although the figure's face was turned away from Jenny, she could glimpse sandaled feet curled up at one end and soft light curls at the other.

Jenny stood frozen.

It had happened too suddenly; she wasn't prepared. She'd seen that dying in the Shadow World didn't mean you got buried and disappeared. She'd known they were looking for Summer, however transformed, however *defiled* Summer might be.

Ever since Michael's dream she'd allowed herself thoughts that Summer might not be lost completely.

But now that she was face to face with the possibility, she couldn't cope with it. She didn't want to go and look, didn't want to *know.* She glanced at the others, saw them standing paralyzed, too.

You have to look. You can take it. It's probably just a normal wax figure with nobody inside. And that's not blood on those spikes, it's red paint.

She knew this was completely irrational. She knew

very well that it probably *wasn't* just a normal wax figure, and that there was no reason for the blood on the spikes to be anything but blood. After everything she'd seen in the Shadow World, after what had happened to Slug and P.C. and her grandfather, she knew that.

But her mind needed to say *something* to get her legs going. To keep away the pictures of Summer's head falling off when Jenny took her by the shoulder, or of some *Rosemary's Baby*–type monster looking up with crafty, glee-filled eyes.

The huge log disk swung on its chain above the table.

I can take it. I can take it. I'm strong enough.

Jenny inched closer. She could see the spun-sugar curls, just the color of Summer's hair, and the little hands lying folded like rose petals. She couldn't see the face.

The log swung, creaking.

With sudden inspiration Jenny thought, *I am my only master.*

She reached for the figure's shoulder.

"Look out!" Dee shouted.

10

There was a clatter above Jenny—the sound of a chain racketing along wood. She reacted instinctively, before rational thought could interfere. She seized the body in the china blue dress and pulled it off the table.

Not fast enough. The huge disk came straight down—and then veered sideways, knocked out of line by something that leaped up by Jenny like black lightning.

Dee hit the disk with both heels, one after the other, so fast that the blows looked simultaneous. The disk swerved, crashing down beside the table. Then the table crashed into Dee, who'd just regained her feet. Dee sprawled on the floor beside Jenny.

The bundle in Jenny's arms stirred.

Shock had wiped all the dreadful thoughts out of her mind, all the pictures of what might be wearing that blue dress. All the fanged, deformed, decayed, or decomposing faces that might have looked up at her from under Summer's fluff of curls.

So it seemed quite natural to see Summer's own small face looking up, with cheeks like rain-washed roses and blinking, sleep-encrusted blue eyes.

Summer yawned and rubbed at her lashes.

"I'm so *tired*—what was the crash?"

Dee had picked herself up and was approaching gingerly. So were Audrey and Michael.

"Is it dead?" Michael said huskily.

Jenny knew what he meant. Just because Summer could talk, that didn't mean she wasn't dead—not here in the Shadow World.

But Summer's weight was warm in Jenny's arms, and Summer's flesh looked like real flesh, not like plastic or that hideous goo that Slug's body had been wearing. Summer looked—alive. Summer looked—all right.

Jenny felt very dizzy.

She couldn't say anything. None of them could. They all just stared at Summer.

Summer's eyes grew large and timid.

"What's wrong?" she said faintly. "What's . . . how long was I asleep?"

Audrey leaned over slowly.

"Summer . . . ?" she whispered, as if she found the word more foreign than any in all the languages she knew.

"What's *wrong?"* Summer wailed.

"How long do you *think* you were asleep?" Michael croaked. "What's the last thing you remember?"

"Well, I was . . . We were all . . ." Summer looked

confused. "Well, I was in that hallway . . . and then you found me . . . and then we went into my bedroom. Only it wasn't my bedroom. And then . . ."

She stopped, her mouth open like a baby bird's.

"Kiddo," Dee said and waved a hand helplessly. "Something bad happened."

"Yeah, but you don't have to think about it."

"I don't *remember* it. Just that it was bad. Did I get hurt? Did I faint?"

Dee looked at Jenny. Jenny looked at Audrey and Michael.

"I think it's really her," Michael said.

"It's her," Dee said. She reached for Summer briskly—almost feverishly, examining Summer's arms and legs. "Are you okay? *Really* okay? Does everything work?"

"Ow."

"Summer," Jenny said abruptly, with a hysterical laugh. She put two fingers to her lips and began crying just as hysterically.

It was catching. Audrey began laughing and crying at the same time. Michael sniffled.

Jenny didn't know what was happening to her. Her heart was skipping—but then it had been skipping all night. She felt dizzy—but she'd been feeling dizzy on and off ever since she'd stepped into the Shadow World.

This was different. It was *like* pain, but it wasn't pain. It coursed through her, flooding up from her toes in an irresistible skyward rush. She actually felt lighter, as if she were lifting toward the ceiling.

All she could think was *oh, thank you.*

Her mind still couldn't get around the concept that

Summer was here, in her own body, talking and moving and apparently well and strong. Not even bruised.

Oh, thank you, thank you.

She had an urge to bundle Summer up and hustle her away somewhere, pack her in tissue paper, keep her safe. Get her to sanctuary before anything else could happen to her.

But there *wasn't* any sanctuary, not here. Summer was alive, but still in danger. She'd have to take her chances like the rest of them.

And anything might happen before they got home.

This thought actually helped Jenny, stopped the giddiness and the trembling inside her. She'd been trying to picture Summer's little brother Cam, with his tough face and his wistful blue eyes, and what he'd look like when he saw his sister again. The picture wouldn't come; it was *too* good, scary good. But now that she realized it might very well never happen, she felt calmer. It seemed more possible now that it was only a possibility.

"I'll *try* to get you out, though," she said, and only realized she'd said it aloud when Summer looked up at her.

"I know you will," Summer said, like a trusting child. "I hate this paper house. Do we look for Zach now? Isn't he next?"

Jenny felt another jolt of improbability as she realized how much they needed to explain to Summer. Wherever Summer had been since they'd last seen her, she obviously didn't remember anything about it.

"Uh, maybe we should talk about that later. Like

when we get outside," Michael said, shooting a pointed glance at Jenny. "This place gives me the creeps."

Yes. They had to get out of this chamber of horrors before any other logs fell on them. The shift to ordinary concerns stopped the last of the trembling inside Jenny. It wasn't that she was less happy—she was *more* happy, now that she was getting over her disbelief. The first joy had been painful, but now a great quietness came over her. Whatever else happened, she could get Summer out of the fun house, to a place where they could rest and talk.

As she stood, helping Dee help Summer up, she saw eyes in the shadows.

Eyes like the ones she'd seen in the mine shaft. They burned with a pale fire. They were watching from the corridor behind Jenny, and they were full of malice.

Jenny slung an arm around Summer's shoulders, turning Summer so she wouldn't see them. "This way."

They won't touch you. I promise. I won't let them.

She meant it. Her happiness wrapped her in a cloak of protection. The Shadow Men could stare all they wanted, but they wouldn't get near Summer.

To her relief, the torture chamber part of the fun house ended with Summer's scene. The narrow corridor wound back and forth a few turns and then opened into a small room with a revolving door and a neon sign that read: EXIT.

"Made it," Dee breathed. Jenny wondered if she had seen the eyes, too.

Summer wriggled out from under Jenny's arm.

"Wait, look at this." Her voice was just as it had always been, light and childish, eager. Jenny could hardly believe she was hearing it again.

Summer was standing in front of a candy machine like the ones Jenny had seen in the arcade. She thrust her small fingers into the one pocket of her shirtdress. "Do any of you guys have a quarter? I'm dying for some chocolate."

"Uh." Michael looked at Jenny. "I don't know if we better . . ."

"We should get out of here," Dee said positively.

"But I'm *starving*. And it'll only take one second—"

Michael looked at Jenny again, and Jenny said, "Oh, give it to her so we can get out," and looked back into the black corridor for the eyes. The candy peanuts had been okay; she supposed this would be. She could hear the sound of Summer putting the quarter in and turning the handle, and then the patter of falling M&M's.

"I hope I didn't get a lot of green ones," Summer said.

Dee said, "I'll open it. Never mind why, Summer."

"Just don't put your hand in," Audrey said, and Jenny turned around in time to see the look Dee gave Audrey.

Then the candies were spilling into Dee's hand—and Dee gave a kind of yelp that made Jenny forget everything and run to her.

Her mind had plenty of time to instantaneously flash over all the horrible things that might have come out of that machine. Dead bugs, red-hot pennies, blobs of acid. Why hadn't she *thought—?* But she was still a step away when she saw the answer gleaming in the pile of candy on Dee's palm.

"Five brown ones, four yellows, two greens, one red, and a gold coin," Michael said coolly, assessing the pile. "Not bad."

Jenny just beat Dee gently on the back.

"Put it somewhere safe," Dee said, and Jenny plucked it from the mound and held it tightly, feeling its coolness before it warmed in her hand. She rubbed her thumb against the engraving. When she opened her hand again, the coin was as rich and shiny as molten gold straight from the forge.

Then she put it in her shirt pocket and buttoned the flap. "Come on, let's go. We did it, we did everything we could here. Summer *and* a coin." She smiled at Summer, who was looking utterly mystified. "We'll explain outside."

Summer accepted the pile of M&M's from Dee and looked somewhat comforted. They all began to go through the revolving door.

It would only take one at a time, and Jenny pushed Summer in front of her. Then she stepped into the next segment of the iron cage and pushed briskly on the thick metal arms, to get out of the fun house as soon as possible. Between the moving arms she could see only darkness—it was pitch black outside, and she couldn't even glimpse Summer's hair. . . .

She knew something was wrong even before she stepped out.

This wasn't the outside. It was a room. And the others weren't with her, because she couldn't see any flashlights.

God, where am I now?

She reached behind her and wasn't at all surprised not to find the iron arms of the revolving door. She was somewhere with no light and no exit.

And now I suppose I see the eyes.

Instead, a small shimmering light went on, and she saw a boy in a black duster jacket.

"Julian?" He looked so different. "Julian!"

Jenny ran toward him, joining him in the shadows. He didn't move an inch to come toward her.

It was the first time she'd ever been glad to see him. But she *was* glad: happiness was blossoming like a flower inside her, petals opening frantically. She stopped in front of him, breathless and triumphant.

"It was you, wasn't it? You gave us Summer back."

"I gave *you* Summer back." His voice was subdued, moody. He was more modestly dressed than Jenny had ever seen him. The black duster jacket wrapped him in shadows.

"Thank you. You don't know—" She paused. Julian probably *did* know. He'd watched Jenny for years; he knew what Summer meant to her. He probably even knew she'd always felt that Summer's death was her fault.

"Is she—okay? Like, really, underneath?" Jenny asked, afraid to say the words, afraid of the answer.

"She's okay. She's been asleep. Just like the princess who pricked her finger on a spindle. Good as new, now." But Julian spoke flatly and he still looked moody. Almost—distrustful.

Jenny ignored it and met the shadowed blue gaze directly.

"Thank you," she said again, very quietly and looking at him so that he could see everything she was feeling.

Julian's heavy lashes drooped, as if he couldn't hold her eyes.

"Julian." Jenny touched both arms of the duster jacket, just below the shoulders. "You did a good thing. You shouldn't act as if you were ashamed."

"I did it for my own reasons." He glanced at her, one quick flash of blue fire, then looked away again.

"Why are you trying to ruin it? You did it, that's what matters." Why couldn't he ever stay the same person twice running? Jenny was thinking. The last time she'd seen Julian he had been subdued and sad—vulnerable. She'd almost felt sorry for him. Now he was cold and sullen—resentful. She wanted to *shake* him.

But she was too scared. You didn't do that to Julian.

"You know," she said, moving in even closer, knowing she was taking a risk, "there was a time when I thought you were completely evil. Completely. But now I don't believe that. I don't think you're as bad as you say you are."

He looked up then, and the blue fire burned steadily. "That's where you're wrong. Don't count on it, Jenny. Don't count on it."

Threads of fear went through her at his voice. It was as musical and cold as she'd ever heard it. The pitiless music of a clear mountain stream that could suddenly rise in a flood and kill everyone in its path.

"I still don't believe it," Jenny breathed. She wouldn't look away from him and she was very close.

"I told you, you're wrong. I am what I am, and nothing can change it." He simply stood there, immovable as rock, which wasn't like Julian at all.

Jenny's fingers clenched on the sleeves of his jacket. "You didn't kill Summer before, in the paper house. You saved her." She rapped out the words as if she were angry.

"Yes." He spoke just as coldly.

"And you *could* have killed her, the rules said you could."

"Yes."

"What about Slug and P.C.?"

He just looked at her.

"Don't play stupid, Julian!" She could have shaken him now, she was angry enough, but instead she stood as rigid and unmoving as he was, their faces inches apart. "Did you kill Slug and P.C.? Make them into what they are now?"

He stared at her a moment, blue eyes unfathomable. Then he said, "Yes."

"You're a damn liar!"

He just looked back at her. His eyes were absolutely bottomless, glacier pools that went down and down forever. Jenny wouldn't look away. She could feel warmth in her own eyes, tears of anger that wouldn't spill.

"Did you do it to Slug and P.C.?" she said, like a TV lawyer prepared to repeat a question endlessly.

Head slightly tilted back, he returned her gaze. Then, face still cold, eyes like blue ice, he said, "No."

His voice was hard and dangerous. Jenny heard her own voice, relentless and just as hard.

"What happened to them?"

"They opened the door to the closet and let me out. But when I *came* out"—a slight and very unsettling smile touched Julian's lips—"they ran. They ran out of the paper house and right into the arms of the other Shadow Men."

Jenny could feel something in her relax slightly, a mystery solved. She wasn't even sure *why* she'd thought Julian hadn't killed P.C. and Slug. He'd always said he had—there was no reason not to believe him. He was a Shadow Man.

But still.

"And they did that?" she asked.

"It was their right. Nobody comes here uninvited."

"And my grandfather. They did that, too." It wasn't a question.

"A long time ago. I didn't pay much attention; I wasn't interested in him. They would never let me touch him. I could keep Summer alive because she was *mine,* my prey that I'd caught myself. And I kept her for a reason, Jenny. To use her against you." His voice was harder than ever, his face like an ice carving.

"But you didn't," Jenny said.

"No. But don't let yourself think that means anything. Next time I will."

"I don't believe you, Julian."

"Then you're making a bad mistake."

There was still no kindness in the midnight blue eyes, nothing to encourage Jenny. Some part of her had the sense to be frightened, but recklessness was flowing through her blood.

There were two sides to Julian, she thought, and

she remembered a line from something she'd read—Emily Brontë, maybe. Different as a moonbeam and lightning.

She wanted to reach the moonbeam part, but she didn't know how.

Very softly she said again, "I don't believe you. You're not like the other Shadow Men. You could change—if you wanted to."

"No," he said bleakly.

"Julian . . ." It was the bleakness that got her. She could see herself reflected in his eyes.

Without thinking, she moved even closer. And closer. Her upper lip touched his lower lip.

"You can change," she whispered.

The kiss began before she knew it. Everything was very sweet. Warmth flowed between the two of them.

Then Julian pulled back. A lock of hair had fallen into his eyes, white as the dogwood blossoms Jenny had seen by the highway. The mask of icy control was broken, but there was something frightening in its place. A kind of shattering.

Like what Jenny had felt herself the last time they kissed, in the cavern with the fire.

She was too excited to dwell on it. She wasn't thinking anymore, only feeling—and she felt hot and victorious. The conqueror. "You're not evil. You *can* change, you can be whatever you want—"

Something ugly sparked in Julian's eyes, the danger and wildness flaming up to overwhelm the shattered light.

"I *am* what I want to be," he said. "You forgot that—and that was your mistake."

"Julian—"

He was flushed, overwrought, his eyes blazing. "You want to see what I really am? I'll show you, Jenny. I'll *prove* it to you. I'll enjoy that."

He spun her around roughly. The revolving door had reappeared, and the neon Exit sign was over it.

"Julian, listen to me—"

From behind, he pushed her toward the door. "Go on, try a little more of the park. See what I've got waiting. *Then* we can talk."

"Julian—" She was frightened, but she turned around as soon as he let go of her.

And of course he wasn't there.

The room was empty. Jenny stood a moment, perfectly still, breathing hard.

He was—he was the most impossible—the most infuriating—

She had never met anyone as—as—

And he *scared* her. She didn't want to try to imagine what he might do next.

Something to prove he was evil, anyway. Something she wouldn't enjoy.

Gradually Jenny's breathing slowed. Summer, she thought. What's important is that I find Summer and get her out of here. No matter what happens, no matter *what,* I have to get Summer out.

Forget about Julian. There's nothing you can do for him. Concentrate on playing his Game and getting out.

Think about *Tom.*

She quashed the guilt that tried to well up then. She *was* thinking about Tom; she wasn't neglecting him. He was in her thoughts all the time, running like an undercurrent beneath whatever else was happening. He was the reason she was still on her feet, still fighting.

She wasn't going to stop until he was safe. Which meant she'd better get moving again right now.

She straightened her shirt, smoothed her hair. Then she stepped into the revolving door's embrace.

11

They were all four waiting for her when she got out.

Summer said, "Where've you *been?*"

Audrey said, "Did you—"

Jenny nodded over Summer's head. Audrey hiked up a copper eyebrow.

"Just a little unscheduled detour," Jenny murmured to Dee and Michael. She said to Summer, "I'm okay. Everything's okay."

Summer's M&M's were lying scattered on the ground. "I don't like people disappearing," she said.

"Aw, honey, it's gonna be all right," Michael said and patted her awkwardly. "We told her where we are and sort of basically what's going on," he said to Jenny.

Jenny's buoyancy at finding Summer was gone; the effervescence had fizzled out of her blood. Julian was going to do something nasty—but what could be worse than what he'd already done? Since she'd known Julian, he'd chased her with UFOs, dark elves, and giant insects—not to mention a Shadow Wolf and Snake. He'd lurked in the shadows of her room and hissed terrifying messages at her in the dark. He'd caught her in a cave-in, left her alone to drown, and menaced her with a cyber-lion. He'd kidnapped her and hunted her throughout two worlds. What could he do to top all that?

"Where do we go next?" Audrey said.

They looked around. Nothing in the immediate vicinity was lit up. The park was completely dark and dead silent around them.

"Here, hold this," Dee said to Jenny.

Jenny took the flashlight and said, "Oh, be *careful.*" Dee was shinning up one of the old-fashioned green-painted lampposts.

"I can see the lighthouse on the island," she said at the top with one long leg hooked over the crosspiece which supported a lantern. "And there're a lot of trees everywhere. . . . The Ferris wheel looks cool, it's sort of rising out of them like a mountain rising out of clouds."

"Is it lit up?"

"The only thing that's lit is something toward the back—it's got a big waterwheel and some boats shaped like swans."

"The Tunnel of Love," Jenny said.

Dee came down and they started toward the Tunnel of Love, Jenny guiding them. It was another ride she'd loved as a kid—not because it had anything to do with love, but because it was dark, and cool, and she'd loved the swan boats. Now, the thought of going into that tunnel was—well, it was better *not* to think about it.

They were skirting the lake when they saw the shape among the trees.

"It's a critter!" Michael said. "Only a big one!"

The flashlight beams caught it briefly, even as it moved back into the trees. It *was* big, and Jenny had a glimpse of reddish skin like tanned leather.

"It's got a head, so it can't be P.C. or Slug," Audrey said.

"Who or who?" asked Summer.

"Never mind. We'd better just watch out for it," Jenny said, and they did, keeping their backs to the water and watching the trees.

I should have asked Julian about them, she thought. Aloud, she said, "What *are* they, d'you think? And how come they're running around loose?"

"Other people the Shadow Men have caught," said Dee.

"Pets," said Michael.

"Or maybe just part of the general *ambiance,"* Audrey said grimly.

Whatever the thing had been, Jenny felt an instinctive horror and revulsion for it, just as she'd felt for the little gray one that had looked like a withered fetus.

Summer didn't join the conversation at all. She just hurried lightly along, one hand gripping Jenny's sleeve, staring at everything they passed. She was like a large blue butterfly skimming in their midst.

They were a motley group, Jenny thought—Summer in her springtime dress and Dee's camouflage jacket, Audrey with her arm tied up in a sling made of Michael's undershirt, Jenny herself carrying

Dee's flashlight. Michael was carrying his own flashlight, while Dee carried Audrey's pick. The other weapons had all gotten lost along the way.

Jenny noticed that Dee kept her distance from Audrey.

Things still weren't right with Dee. She was too quiet, too un-exuberant. Sure they were in danger, but Dee *loved* danger, she got up and ate it for breakfast, breathed it, went looking for it whenever she could. Dee should be enjoying this.

Jenny edged closer and said softly, "You know, Audrey didn't mean anything by that—when she said not to put your hand in the M&M's machine."

Dee shrugged. "I know." She went on looking straight ahead.

"Really she didn't. She's just like my mom, sometimes she's got to say things for your own good."

"Sure. I know."

Jenny gave up.

They passed a food stand just before they got to the Tunnel of Love. Jenny had an urge to break in—even a cold hot dog would be good right now, even a bun—but she didn't say anything. They had two gold coins. They were so close. They couldn't stop for anything now.

Blue and red and purple lights shone on the waterwheel in front of the Tunnel of Love. There was a rustic old mill behind the waterwheel, and a sign on the tunnel. In the afternoon, in the real park, the sign had read: TUNNEL OF LOVE. Now it read: TUNNEL OF LOVE AND D—.

The last word was obscured by clusters of ivy. "I can't read it," Jenny said.

"Death, probably. As in 'Love and death are the only two things that really matter.' *N'est-ce pas?*" Audrey said.

"Oh, spiffy," said Michael. Summer got a firmer grip on Jenny's sleeve.

A swan boat was waiting at the loading dock, its white wings arched gracefully by its sides, its neck a supple curve. Beads of water glistened on the plastic. Jenny didn't want to get into it.

If that head turns around—

But they didn't have any choice. This was obviously the right place, awake and waiting for them. If Jenny wanted the third gold coin, she had to get on the ride.

"Come on, people," she said.

The boat tilted as they got in—Jenny and Dee on the front seat with Summer between them, Audrey and Michael in the back. They sat on wooden boards. As soon as they were all in, the swan began to move.

"Did you notice that cave looking like a face this afternoon?" Michael said as they approached the tunnel.

Jenny hadn't. The fiberglass rock *did* look like a face now, with crags and shadows forming the eyes and nose. The gaping mouth was the tunnel itself.

Inside, it was dank and dark, with a musty smell. And quiet. That afternoon there had been the sounds of people talking, the occasional echoing laugh. Now all Jenny could hear was the quiet lapping of water around the boat.

She was still holding the flashlight Dee had given her, and she trained it on the water, the walls, the swan's head. All unexciting. The water was dark green and murky, the walls were damp and trickly, the swan's head was staying put.

"Where's the stuff—the scenes and everything?" Michael whispered. It was a whispering kind of place.

"I don't know," Jenny said, just as softly. That afternoon there had been illuminated dioramas—silly things like Stone Age people playing cards and painting dinosaurs on the cave walls. Now there was nothing. The swan boat went on gliding smoothly into darkness.

That was when Jenny noticed something wrong with the flashlight. The light was getting dimmer.

"Hey," she said and turned it toward her. Orange. The white beam was receding into a sullen orange glow.

She banged it on the swan's neck and immediately wished she hadn't. It made a startlingly loud sound, and the light got even dimmer.

"Oh, criminy—mine, too," Michael said. She could hear the jingle of metal as he shook it.

"We should have kept just one on, to save the batteries," Dee muttered. "I *thought* of that before, and then I forgot. I'm *stupid.*"

Even in the midst of her worry Jenny was shocked at this. Dee didn't talk that way. "Look, Dee, if anybody should have thought of it—"

"There it goes," Michael said. There was now complete darkness from the backseat. Jenny had been thumbing the switch of her flashlight and screwing and unscrewing the top, but it didn't make any difference. She could barely see the dim orange bulb. When she shook it, it went out altogether.

"Spiffy, spiffy, spiffy," Michael said.

Audrey said sharply, "Does anybody feel like we're slowing down?"

It was hard to tell in the dark. Jenny was thoroughly sick of darkness—it seemed as if she'd spent all night blind, wondering what might be coming at her from which direction.

But she thought Audrey could be right. The lapping water was quieter. The only motion she could feel was the gentle swaying of the boat from side to side.

There was a quiet splash. "We're not moving," Dee said.

"Dee, get your hand out of the water!"

Dee muttered something inaudible, but Jenny heard the drip as she took her hand out.

"I don't *like* this," Summer said.

Jenny didn't, either—and she especially didn't like the thought of getting out of the boat and sloshing around trying to find their way.

"So we're stranded," she murmured. Everyone else was very still and tense.

Wondering what's coming at us, and from which direction. . . .

She could think of lots of things, all of them nasty. And she had time to think, because for a long while they just sat there, the swan boat rocking gently in the darkness.

"Just don't imagine anything," Audrey said through her teeth from the backseat.

"I'm *trying* not to," Michael answered defensively.

But of course it was impossible, like trying *not* to think of a pink elephant. The harder Jenny tried not to imagine what Julian might do to them, the quicker the images crowded into her mind. Every nightmare she'd ever had was suddenly clamoring for her attention.

"I can't take this anymore," Summer breathed.

Dee exhaled sharply. "No. Look, I'm gonna—"

Light.

It started as a fuzzy blue patch in Jenny's peripheral vision, and brightened when she turned to look at it. Like a spotlight in some overly dramatic stage show. Two other spotlights went on, one red, one purple. The colors of the floodlights outside—and the colors of the stained-glass lamps in the More Games shop, Jenny thought. The place where she'd first seen Julian.

"It all comes down to this, doesn't it?" Julian's voice said.

He moved out of the darkness, into the circle where the spotlights mingled. He was wearing a T-shirt with rolled-up sleeves, a black vest, and neat black boots. There was some kind of bangle around his upper arm. He looked urban and barbaric, like somebody you might find wandering the bad parts of town at night. Some street kid with no place to go and too much knowledge behind his blue eyes.

Summer took one look at him and crouched behind Dee.

Jenny felt at a disadvantage. Julian was in the place where the diorama should be—but she felt as if the five of them in the flimsy plastic boat were the show. Julian was in a perfect position to watch whatever happened to them—and they couldn't even stand without risking an upset.

"You were wrong about the sign on this ride," Julian said casually. He stood easily, seeming to enjoy their reactions as they stared at him. "It's not the Tunnel of Love and Death. It's the Tunnel of Love—and Despair."

The five in the boat just looked at him. Finally Dee said, "So what?"

"Just thought you'd like to know." He flipped something in the air, caught it. Jenny couldn't tell what color the thing was because of the lights, but it gleamed.

"What, this? Oh, yes, it's a doubloon," Julian said, looking into his palm as if only just then noticing it.

Everyone in the boat exchanged glances. The boat rocked gently.

"Don't you want to know what you have to do to get it?"

Jenny didn't, but she felt sure he was going to tell them anyway.

"You just have to listen, that's all. We'll have a little conversation. A chat."

It was up to Jenny to answer, and she knew it. "About what?" she said tensely, leaning back to look at him around Dee.

"This and that. The weather. Nuclear disarmament. You."

"Us?" Michael squeaked, startled into speech.

"Sure. Look at you—all of you. What a pathetic bunch. And *you're* trying to storm the Shadow World?"

"Right," Dee muttered and started to get up.

"You never learn, do you?" Julian said and took a step toward her.

That was all he did, but Dee sat down, only partly because Jenny had grabbed her arm and pulled her back. Julian was scaring Jenny right now—not with any overt display of power, but just with *himself*. What he was. Julian picked up moods and put them on like clothes, and right now the brightness in his eyes, the quick rise of his breathing, the way his lips were slightly skinned back from his teeth—they all scared Jenny. He was in the mood to destroy things, to bring down some ultimate disaster, she thought. Not just to hunt, but to kill.

"Please, let's all just be calm," she said.

Julian was still looking at Dee, with bright sickness shining in his eyes. "Maybe you're just too *stupid* to learn," he said. "That's the real reason you don't want to go to college, isn't it? You know you'll never be as smart as your mother."

"Don't rise to him," Jenny said. "Dee, turn around—just don't listen."

Dee didn't turn. Jenny could only see her silhouette, and the blue light glistening on the velvet nubs of hair on her head, but she could *feel* the stress in Dee's body.

"All this athletic stuff is just a front because you know you've disappointed her," Julian said. "You're inferior where it counts most."

"Dee, you *know* that's not true. . . ."

"She knows she doesn't know *anything*. She's been wrong about so many things recently—like about Audrey and the lion. Like about Audrey's mother.

Imagine *Mrs. Myers* having done something Dee always meant to do."

"You leave her alone!" Jenny said.

"And she's nothing without her confidence. Haven't you noticed?"

"Shut up!" Dee shouted. It was a bad place for shouting, there were distant echoes. What frightened Jenny was the note of desperation in Dee's voice. Dee never cried, but just now Dee's voice sounded on the verge of tears.

"Despair," Jenny whispered suddenly. She reached around Dee to grip her arm. "Don't you see what he's trying to do? The Tunnel of Love and Despair—and he wants *you* to despair. To give up, to stop fighting."

"She should give up," Julian agreed. He was breathless now, the queer wild look in his eyes brighter than ever. "She's all talk. Hot air. Strutting around, building her muscles, saying 'Everybody look at me.' But there's nothing underneath."

Jenny thought of something. She leaned in toward Dee, her fingers biting into Dee's arm, and said, *"I am my only master."*

Dee's head turned slightly, like a startled bird.

"I am my only master," Jenny whispered urgently, prompting her. "Go on, Dee. You said it, and it's true. He can't do anything to you. He doesn't count. You are your only master."

She felt Dee's breath go out.

"Gets her philosophy from kung fu movies," Julian said. "Thinks fortune cookies are great literature."

"I am my only master!" Dee said.

"That's right." Jenny's throat hurt. She kept holding on to Dee's arm. Dee's neck twisted like a black swan's, to look at Jenny just for a moment. Jenny got a glimpse of tear tracks on the dark skin, shining blue and purple in the light, then Dee turned back.

"I am my only master," she said clearly, to Julian.

There was a stirring in the backseat. "She's smart, too," Audrey said, astonishing Jenny. "And brave. She's done all sorts of brave things since I got hurt. She didn't mean to hurt me, and I never thought she did."

Dee turned and gave Audrey one sloe-eyed look of gratitude, and her shoulders straightened. She sat as proud and tall as Nefertiti.

"Besides, college and books aren't everything," Michael said, amazing Jenny further.

"I thought they were—to *you,*" Julian said. He was looking at Michael now, and his voice was beautiful, like ebony and silver.

Michael seemed to get smaller.

"You're the one who reads about things because you're afraid to actually do them. You talk about your books—or make jokes. The class clown. But people are laughing *at* you, not with you, you know."

"No, they're not," Michael said, which was another surprise for Jenny. She wouldn't have thought Michael would speak up for himself.

"You're a nothing. Just a funny little fat boy that people laugh at. You're a joke."

"No, I'm not," Michael said doggedly. Jenny felt a surge of admiration. Michael was holding out—maybe *because* he'd gotten teased and stomped on at school. He'd heard it all before.

But Julian's face was more confident than ever—and more cruel. He flashed a smile that sent chills up Jenny's arms.

"We won't talk about the little rituals you had when you were a kid," he told Michael. "Like how you had to tear the toilet paper up into tiny pieces, exactly even. Or if you saw the word *death,* you had to count to eighteen. To *chai*—'life' in Hebrew."

Michael's chest was heaving. Jenny opened her mouth, outraged, but Julian went urbanely on.

"We'll just cut to the chase. Ask your girlfriend if she's ever called you 'Tubby' behind your back."

Michael turned on Audrey. Jenny could see that his defenses had torn; his face had that rumpled, not-ready-for-company look that meant he was about to cry. "Did you say that?"

Audrey looked pale in the blue and purple lights, her lipstick garish. She seemed ready to cry, too.

"Did you say that?"

"Of course she did," Julian said. "She said lots of other things, too. About how her dream boy was six feet tall and blond and a surfer. About how she only took up with you to fill in the time until she found someone better."

Michael was looking at Audrey. "Did you say that?" he repeated, his voice an anguished plea.

Jenny willed Audrey to say no. Audrey looked back at Michael for a long, horrible moment, then said, "Yes."

Michael turned away.

"Because you were good for a laugh," Julian put in helpfully. "Don't you want to laugh now?"

"Shut up, you bastard!" Jenny shouted furiously.

She was sick with her own impotence—she'd helped Dee, but there was nothing she could do to help Michael. Not with this.

"I told you in the very beginning about the Game," Julian said. "Desires unveiled. Secrets revealed. Don't you remember?"

Audrey wasn't listening, she was looking only at Michael, her whole being focused on him. "I did say that," she said fiercely. "A long time ago. I didn't even really mean it then, I was just showing off."

"You still said it," Michael said dully, not turning.

"I said it *before,* Michael. Before you showed me that what people look like isn't important. Before I found out I loved you." She dissolved in sobs.

Michael turned halfway. His dark eyes were wide open.

"Oh—look," he said. "Don't. It's okay."

"It's *not* okay," Audrey stormed. "Michael Allen Cohen—you're an idiot!"

"That's what *he* said—" Michael muttered. Audrey shook him, turning him the rest of the way around.

"I *love* you," she said. "You made me fall in love with you. I don't care how tall you are or what color your hair is—I care about *you.* You make me laugh. You're smart. You're gentle. And you're *real,* you're a real person, not some jock with a facade that's going to fall apart when I get to know him. I know you already, and I love you, you idiot. I don't care what you do with toilet paper."

"When I was *seven,"* Michael said. Audrey was still crying, and he reached out a stubby thumb to wipe the tears off her cheeks.

"You're a good kisser, too," Audrey said, sniffling. She put her arms around him and laid her head on his shoulder.

"Hey, I'm a *great* kisser," Michael whispered. "As I will demonstrate when we get out of this freakin' freak show." He cradled her protectively.

Jenny felt a flush of pride and joy—in their strength, in the tenderness in Michael's face and the way Audrey clung to him.

She looked at Julian defiantly.

Julian wasn't happy. He obviously didn't like the way things were going. Then he smiled, sharp as a sword.

"That's right, cry, you whining baby," he said, his eyes fixed on Audrey's auburn head. "But make sure you don't smear your mascara. You're nothing but a painted mannequin." His voice was venomous.

"We're not listening!" Michael said. He began talking to Audrey, softly and rapidly, right in her ear.

"You're going to turn out like your mother, you know—a shrill and contentious bitch. Your father's words, I believe. You're afraid that you're not capable of having real feelings like other people."

Audrey didn't even lift her head. Michael went on talking to her.

"I'd say she's doing a pretty good imitation of having feelings," Dee said dryly. "Why don't you just back off, creep?"

Instead, Julian whirled on her—no, not on her. He was looking behind her, at Summer. "And as for the brainless bit of fluff in front—"

Summer collapsed onto the floor of the boat. "I know I'm stupid," she whispered.

Jenny's fury lifted her to her feet, making the swan boat rock.

"Oh, no, you don't," she said. "If you have something to say, say it to *me.*"

And then she was doing what she'd *least* wanted to do all this time. She was getting out of the boat, splashing down into the water.

It was cool, but it only came up to her knees. She splashed through it without letting herself think what might be swimming in it. Waves churned up, wetting her thighs.

She reached the diorama in a few steps and scrambled up on it. Then she was facing Julian.

"Say it to *me,*" she said. "If you have the guts."

12

I'm the one all this is for," Jenny said. "It's me you want to despair. So talk to *me*. Let's get personal."

"No, let's get general," Julian said. "Want to talk about life?"

There was a kind of soft triumph in his voice. A cat-pouncing-on-a-mouse tone. As if he knew he had her.

"Did you know," he went on, "that in the Congo there's a kind of fly that lays its eggs in human flesh? They develop into little white worms that live inside you forever. Sometimes the worms surface and you can watch them crawling inside the skin of your arm. They say that when they crawl inside your eyeball it's quite painful."

Jenny stood where she was, appalled.

"That's Nature for you," Julian said and laughed. The laugh didn't sound quite sane.

Jenny got her voice back. "We're not worms."

"No. Humans are a lot more inventive. Mustard gas, for instance. It touches you, your skin comes rolling off. Happened to thousands of soldiers in World War I. Some man invented that for the benefit of his brothers."

Jenny wanted to look away from Julian, but she couldn't. The spotlights threw swaths of red and purple on his hair. His eyes were mirror-brilliant.

"It's the same all down through history. Two million years ago your hominid ancestors were eating each other. In thirteenth-century Peru they used to crack little boys' ribs wide open so the priests could take their hearts out still beating. These days it's drive-by shootings. People never change."

Jenny could feel her breath catch. "Okay . . ."

The soft, insidious voice went on. "So Nature is cruel and ruthless."

"Okay . . ."

"And life is fragile and bewildering. And death—death is inevitable and worse than anything you can imagine."

From the boat Dee said defiantly, "Who cares?"

Julian spoke without turning toward Dee. *"She* cares," he said. "Don't you, Jenny? You care if it's a cruel and pointless universe. You care if you're surrounded by evil."

There was something almost mesmeric about his gaze now. His voice was reasonable, flowing. "So why not despair? There's nothing wrong with that. Things will be so much easier once you've given up. Why not just relax and give in. . . ."

He was coming toward her, and Jenny knew she

couldn't resist. He was coming to put a warm palm on the back of her neck, maybe, or press her hand. And whatever he did, she wouldn't be able to resist, because at that moment his beauty was so unearthly it was frightening.

"I believe you!" she said, speaking before he got to her. He stopped, head tilted slightly, quizzically. Then suddenly she was speaking in a rush. "You wanted to prove how much evil there is—well, fine; I believe you. And I don't know all the answers. I don't even know the stupid *questions*. But not everything is evil, like you say. There are good people. Like Aba. Like my grandfather. He died to save me, and he's not the only person who's died for somebody else. I can't explain the evil that's out there, but that doesn't mean I ought to *join* it. It doesn't mean I should give in."

The smiling victory had drained out of Julian's face, and something cold and ugly was rising in his eyes instead. But Jenny went on before he could speak, her words tumbling over one another. "You said I cared about whether it was a cruel and pointless universe, and I do. But you want to know something else I care about? I care about you, Julian."

He was startled now. He looked as if he might almost take a step backward. Because Jenny was moving forward, deliberately, holding his eyes and speaking.

"You wanted to show me how it's all right to be evil, because everything else is that way. But I'm not buying it. And you wanted to prove to me how bad you are, but I'm not buying that, either. I care about *you,* Julian. I—"

He disappeared just as she reached him.

The gold coin fell spinning to the ground.

Jenny picked it up a moment or so later, after standing quite still and watching it spin on its side for a while and finally land flat. Looking toward the boat, she saw that they were all looking at *her:* Dee, and Audrey, and Michael—and Summer, who was just poking her head out. Nobody seemed to know what to say.

It's not what you think, Jenny thought, but she didn't know how to explain it to them. She *did* care about Julian. She'd seen the moonbeam side of him, the vulnerable side that was so badly hurt it made him strike out. She even . . . loved Julian . . . in a way she was just discovering. But that didn't mean she didn't love Tom. Tom was a part of her life, a part of *her.* She could never betray him.

But putting all that in words was beyond her. They'd just have to think whatever they wanted.

"You know," Michael said at last, running a hand through his rumpled dark hair, "I think we just won this Game." He smiled, a weak and wry smile, but a real one nevertheless.

"And I think we should get out of here on foot," Dee said. "My guess is this boat isn't moving."

Nobody talked much as they sloshed through the tunnel. Dee went first, one hand on the dank wall to guide her. Jenny followed with Summer, and Audrey and Michael brought up the rear, holding hands. Jenny had the feeling that they were all sore from

Julian's last and most terrible attack—but they were stronger for it, too. In the end it had pulled them together. Julian had revealed their secrets—and Jenny had never felt so close to her friends before.

She was relieved to see Dee's form silhouetted against lighter blackness and to feel fresh air on her face. They had found the end of the tunnel. Now she could see the loading dock.

"Will you look at this!" Michael exclaimed when they reached it and climbed up. "Will you just look, please?"

The park was awake.

All the lights that had been off were on, and all the rides were going. Fairy lights twinkled and glimmered in the trees, white lights played on a fountain below them. To the left, the Turnpike was illuminated, with lines of sports cars standing ready to race. Straight ahead, the rocket ride was already in motion, red-lit rockets up and whizzing. The structure of the March Hare roller coaster was picked out in flashing neon, and Jenny could hear the clatter of a car on the wooden tracks.

Everything was going, all at once. It looked exactly like a normal amusement park at night—except that it was still deserted. The rides were operating by themselves.

Beautiful, Jenny thought, but scary. As if the whole park was inhabited by ghosts. The merry-go-round music was distant but eerily distinct, and she could hear the Noah's Ark foghorn in the pauses.

On the central island of the lake, the lighthouse rose white and slender and silent.

"Now we find the bridge, I suppose," Audrey said quietly from behind Jenny.

Jenny unbuttoned her shirt pocket, reached in. She looked at the three doubloons on her palm, felt their satisfying weight. Then she closed her hand and heard them clink softly.

"There's something we have to do first," she said. "Follow me."

The arcade was only a short distance away. Its sign was lighted, too, but the inside was dim and quiet. Jenny went straight to the cabinet with the mechanical wizard.

She tried not to look at the black cabinet that stood opposite, but she got a glimpse of the heads anyway. They were as blue and ghastly as ever, their eyes still shut. Jenny turned her back on them firmly and faced the wizard.

He was moving just the tiniest bit. As if some battery were running down. His hand lifted the wand and dropped it slightly, lifted and dropped, a sad repetitive motion. His head bobbed just as slightly, the dark marble eyes staring out into nothingness. Every so often his lower lip moved.

"Grandfather," Jenny said.

It was a formal moment, and *Grandpa* didn't seem quite right. He was Grandfather, like all the Grandfathers in fairy tales, a mystical, archetypical figure. Someone who belonged in a story.

Dee had said there was nothing Jenny could do for him, and it was true. She'd accepted it before, really, and she was even more certain now. There was no way to put his soul back into his body—if he even had a body anymore, which Jenny doubted. No way to fix him or undo what the Shadow Men had done.

But there was one thing she might be able to do. It had come to her while she was talking to Julian, surging up in the back of her mind when she had said that her grandfather had died for her. He hadn't—exactly—but he'd meant to. And she was sure he'd rather be dead than be like this.

The only question was whether her idea would work.

"Grandfather, I thought of something, something from your journal. A way to help you. But I need to know if it will work—and if it's what you want."

The matted-paintbrush eyelashes seemed to droop, then lift. The glass eyes didn't look at her, and the ruddy plastic face couldn't change expression. But she had the feeling he was listening.

"I saw the runes in your journal, and I know that runes can do things here, they can change reality. They can make things happen. And the rune I'm thinking of is Gebo, Grandfather, do you understand? Gebo."

"What's she *talking* about?" Summer whispered, from several steps away, where the others waited.

"I don't know. Gebo—which was that?" Dee said, and Michael said, "Shush, okay?"

Jenny stood watching the mechanical figure in the black velveteen robe, and waiting.

Suddenly the glass eyes rolled. The whole figure moved jerkily, banging the wand up and down. The carmine lips opened and shut, and the head bobbed.

It was a perfect frenzy of motion, like a mute

person in a straitjacket trying desperately to convey agreement. At least, that was what Jenny hoped it was. If she was wrong, it was going to be a terrible mistake.

"All right," she whispered. "I love you, Grandpa." She could feel tears starting in her eyes, but she wasn't going to cry, she wasn't. She wasn't really sad. She was happy and a little scared. Beyond all hope, she'd gotten to see her grandfather again. It had helped her remember him, how kind he'd been to her, how much he'd loved her—whatever his other faults. She'd gotten the chance to say she was sorry, and now she had the chance to say goodbye. It was more than a lot of people got, more than Jenny could ever have expected.

She reached into her back pocket for the Swiss Army knife.

It had been there all along, almost forgotten since she'd tucked it away in the mine ride. It had survived the cave-in and the flood and everything else. She was glad, because it was Tom's, and now because it was very useful.

She held it in her hand a moment, then thumbed open the large blade. She set the blade against the old-fashioned wooden cabinet, just above the glass, and, bearing down hard, carved a diagonal stroke. Then she made another that crossed the first in the middle, forming an *X*. Making Gebo, the rune of sacrifice. It was funny, how she'd had a premonition about that when they were carving it on the door. She'd felt that it had been important somehow—but she'd never imagined this.

She stepped back.

Pinching her left index finger between middle finger and thumb, she watched the end go purple with blood. Then, without hesitation, she jabbed once with the knife.

She didn't really know whether she needed blood for this. Isa, the ice rune she'd used to stop the flooding waterfall, had worked without it. But she wanted to do this just right, and make absolutely sure.

Squeezing the finger, she painted the *X* with blood. Then she stepped back again.

The mechanical figure was perfectly still, as if waiting. Everything seemed to be waiting, the universe holding its breath around Jenny. For a moment she was afraid she couldn't speak, but the dark eyes were at last looking straight at her. There was a silent encouragement in them, almost a plea. And a gentle trust.

The third step is to say the name of the rune out loud.

Jenny took a deep breath and clearly and quietly said, "Gebo."

Rune of sacrifice, of death. Of yielding up the spirit.

It happened immediately, startling her. The figure in the cabinet, the mechanical thing dressed in black velveteen and gold sequins, spasmed as if a jolt of electricity had gone through it. Both arms jerked up, the head rolled wildly. Cracks ran along the caked paint on its face, flaking off in pieces. Every part of the figure that could move thrashed frantically.

And then the clenched fist with the wand fell. The entire figure sagged, its head falling back. It was as if some mainspring had been sprung, or the wires to a marionette cut. The carmine lips were slightly open.

Jenny, scarcely breathing, stared at the face.

It—had changed. It was still plastic—cracked and peeling plastic. It was clearly a broken doll.

But—the pain was gone. The look that had wrenched Jenny's heart in the beginning, the look of ineffable sadness, wasn't there anymore. The carmine lips seemed to be smiling slightly, and the glass eyes, though open, seemed at peace.

There was an odd dignity that went with the peace. The face was patient and almost noble, for all that it was a doll's face. Whatever her grandfather had done, whatever secrets he'd meddled in, he'd paid the price—and this doll seemed to know it. Its expression was that of somebody who'd waited a long time to get to the end of a journey, and was home at last.

"You can rest now," Jenny said, and then she had to wipe her eyes on her denim sleeve.

A click made her look down. A fortune-telling card was in the slot.

Jenny took it, turned it over. There were only two words in the middle.

THANK YOU.

Then she really did cry, looking around as if her grandfather's soul might be floating somewhere in the room where she could see it. Wherever it had gone, it was free.

"What about *them?*" Dee said. Jenny looked at the others and saw that they were sniffling, too—and Dee was looking at the black cabinet.

Jenny wiped her eyes again, and her nose, and then she made herself look. Slug and P.C. were more hideous than ever because they were awake.

Their eyes followed her with the desperate longing of dogs that wanted to go out on a walk. Neither of them had been particularly handsome when they were alive, and in death they were grotesque. Jenny swallowed.

"Can you hear me?"

The two grisly objects bobbed.

"Did you see what I did?"

Bob. Bob.

"Do you—do you want me to do it for you?"

Bob, bob, bob, bob, bob, bob, bob . . .

Jenny burst into tears and went on crying as she lifted the knife. She *needed* to cry. She had never liked either of these guys; they'd stalked her on an empty street, they'd meant to do her harm, they'd broken into her house and stolen from her. And now they looked like those little dogs with nodding heads that people put in the back of their cars, and Jenny was going to kill them.

She went on sobbing as she carved the two *X*s, one over each head, and stabbed her middle finger. She was still crying as she began to stain the first *X* red.

So she didn't notice the attack until Dee started shouting.

Jenny looked up and froze. It was another body like the one that had grabbed Dee at the Fish Pond, and it had the same ghastly emptiness above its shoulders. The only difference was that it wasn't white and bloated, and it was wearing a black T-shirt and leather vest. It was P.C.

In the cabinet the head with the black bandanna was shaking violently—as if to disassociate itself with the lumbering body that Dee was fighting. Its eyes were terrified, straining sideways to try and watch.

"I think the Shadow Men must control the bodies!" Michael shouted, pulling Summer out of the way. Audrey had stumbled back, too, and Dee was fighting the thing alone, swinging Audrey's pick. Cabinets on both sides were smashing.

Jenny, caught completely unprepared, was still frozen.

"Come on, hurry!" Michael shouted. He grabbed the knife from her hand and stabbed his own finger. The next thing she knew he was staining the other rune, making sharp, slashing motions on the cabinet.

"Come on, Jenny!"

Trancelike, Jenny raised her finger, smearing pale red across the second stroke of the *X*. The headless body had gotten hold of Dee's pick and was jerking it away from her, pulling her within range.

Jenny whirled back to the cabinet, energized. The blue-lit heads gazed at her, looking imploring and stupid and more pathetic than anything she'd ever seen.

"Gebo!" she shouted.

Michael shouted it, too, maybe because his blood was in the runes. Then several things happened in quick succession.

Both the heads in the box jerked. Their jaws fell open, impossibly far open, revealing blue-stained teeth. Their eyes rolled up. And there was a noise—an inhuman howling that seemed to come from all around Jenny rather than from the open jaws. Down the corridor there was a terrible crashing.

P.C.'s body was flailing with the pick, breaking glass and splintering wood. As Jenny watched he flailed more and more jerkily, then stopped. His body flopped backward, collapsing like a pricked balloon.

Meanwhile, from every side, there was clicking and whirring and plinking music. The entire arcade had come to life at once. The foot vitalizer was vibrating. In a shattered cabinet a mechanical ballerina was twirling. The figures in the Ole Barn Dance were clacking their wooden jaws.

"Let's get the hell out of here!" Dee shouted over the music of a nickelodeon.

Jenny cast one last glance at the black cabinet. The heads were still now, and she supposed their blank and empty expressions were peaceful. Certainly nobody was *in* there anymore.

Then she was moving, stepping over glass shards and P.C.'s motionless body, while the arcade gibbered and screeched around her. A minute later she was in the open air.

It was an unspeakable relief to get away from the

noise. The outside seemed clean somehow, even if it was in the Shadow World.

She looked at Dee. "Are you okay?"

"Yeah." Dee was gripping her thigh with both hands, pulling bits of glass out of her jeans. "I got some shrapnel here, but I'm all right."

Jenny looked at Summer, who was huddling and hugging her own elbows. "Are *you* all right?"

Summer managed an extremely watery smile.

"I got splinters," Michael offered, holding up his finger.

"That was brave of you," Jenny said. She was remembering the way he'd looked in her grandfather's house when she had first explained that they needed to stain the runes with blood.

Michael just looked at her. "Huh?"

"Never mind. Summer, give Dee back her jacket. Audrey, are you okay to walk? Because I have the feeling we'd better keep moving. I think they're mad."

She squeezed her shirt pocket and felt the reassuring heaviness there. She felt the need to hurry, as if a storm were gathering behind her. The Shadow Men weren't happy with what she'd done to their prisoners.

"Wait, but how do we find the bridge?" Michael said.

"We'll just walk around the lake until we see it."

They saw it as soon as they cleared the trees by the Penny Arcade. It started somewhere in between the March Hare roller coaster and the Log Ride, rising in a beautiful arch like a rainbow that ended on the island.

"I don't *think* that was there before," Audrey said.

"Maybe it just wasn't lit," Dee said.

Michael said, "It's going to be like climbing the St. Louis Arch."

Everybody looked at Jenny.

"We'll do it," she said stoutly. "We *have* to. We have to get to Tom and Zach—and *quick,* because they may try to stop us or something. We've got to actually get to them to win the Game."

"I don't see how the coins fit in," Dee muttered.

But when they reached the nearer base of the arch, Jenny saw. There was a neat little tollbooth in front of it, and a fence with barbed wire that kept you from climbing up the sides. After the first ten feet it was so high in the air that you couldn't have reached the side if you had wanted to.

"What holds it up?" Summer whispered, and Jenny said, "Don't ask."

Attached to the white tollbooth was a coin receiver with a flat tray—like the kind you see in airports for getting luggage carts. Instead of four spaces for quarters there were three spaces for irregularly shaped coins in the tray. With a little twisting and exchanging, Jenny got all three gold pieces to fit neatly. They lay there and gleamed at her.

She looked at the others.

It was a momentous moment, a serious, *profound* moment. They'd finished the treasure hunt and they were about to go collect the prize. She felt as if somebody ought to make a significant gesture.

"Dee? You want to push it? Or Audrey?"

"You earned it, Sunshine. Go on and make it happen," Dee said.

Jenny was happy.

She pushed the tray in and felt it lock in place. The white-and-yellow striped turnstile lifted.

"After you," she said and gestured the others through.

13

Dee took the lead, with Summer following her lightly and Michael and Audrey after that.

Jenny wanted the others to go ahead of her partly because she was afraid, and partly because she didn't want any of them trying to save her if she fell off.

Heights. She had always hated heights. But she was *damned* if she was going to let this bridge stop her from getting to Tom.

It wasn't all that bad at the beginning. Steep, yes, and narrow, yes. And there were no handrails. If the whole structure had been six inches off the ground, Jenny could have walked it easily, without a chance of slipping. The problem was doing it twenty feet off the ground.

But if she looked straight down and concentrated on her own feet, she couldn't see how they were climbing.

Just then, though, something drifted past her

feet—a wisp of mist. Alarmed, she looked to one side.

No, they weren't cloud-height. They really were only twenty feet off the ground. But mist was rising around them.

"Oh, *spiffy,"* Michael said from somewhere ahead, and Summer's voice said, "I can't *see."*

Dee's voice floated back from even farther ahead. "Reach back and hold hands with each other. I can feel my way along."

Jenny reached forward and took a handful of Audrey's nylon jacket—Audrey only had one good arm to use. She shuffled forward, gritting her teeth. Everything around her was white. She could barely see her own hiking boots.

In a few minutes, though, her head broke through the mist. She went on shuffling upward, inching out of it. Her legs were aching, and she hoped they were getting near the top.

It was only when Audrey stopped short in front of her, and gasped, that she looked around.

The mist was gone. What she saw beneath the bridge now was—unearthly.

It was dark, and arching through the darkness were other bridges, delicate and airy, some fiery, some that looked like ice. They led to clumps of land that looked like islands floating in space.

"Like Neverland," Jenny whispered. "A bunch of Neverlands. What *are* they? And where are *we?"*

"Oh, I don't believe this," Audrey said just as softly.

"I do," Dee said from the very top of the arch. Her

head was thrown back on the slim dark column of her neck. Faint light from the bridges shifted on the planes of her cheekbones, and her eyes glowed. "I do."

Some of the islands were brighter and more substantial-looking than any landscape Jenny had seen on Earth—sharper in detail, more exquisite in clarity. Others were dim and vague—as if they had been partly formed and then abandoned.

Between the clumps of land Jenny could see stars—but not normal stars. These stars rippled and waved as if she were looking at them through a clear stream, or as if they were studded on a flowing length of black silk. There was something incredibly lost and lonely about them.

"But what *are* those things? Those other islands?" she said again.

Audrey gave herself a little shake and seemed to focus. "I think—those are the nine worlds. From Norse mythology—Norse, like the runes. I told you about them once."

"You mean—we're *above* the Shadow World somehow?"

"I guess. Now that—that's probably Asgard, the one way up there. It's got to be."

Jenny tilted her head back. Far above them—the farthest away of any of the clumps—was an island world that seemed all silver and gold. She could just glimpse something like a shining mountain rising into a golden cloud on it. The bridge to it was very narrow and seemed to be on fire.

"That's where the gods live."

"The gods?" Jenny spoke to Audrey without looking down from the shining island.

"So the myths say. Hmm, and I'll bet *that's* Vanaheim. World of primal water and plenty, where some of the less important gods live." Audrey pointed to an island painted in jewel-like colors, dark blue and dark green.

"Vanaheim—any relation to Anaheim?" Michael murmured. Audrey pinched her mouth on a smile, but ignored him.

"And that's Alfheim, world of light and air," she said, nodding at an island that was much closer to them, shimmering in the colors of sunrise: yellow, pale blue, light green. "Home of light elves—like good spirits. I'm remembering all this, isn't that amazing? I must have been about eight when I learned it."

"What about those?" Dee said, pointing straight outward. Two island worlds were floating at about the same level as the bridge they stood on: one rocky and lashed by what looked like tornadoes, and the other so bright with orange fire that Jenny couldn't make out any details.

"The rocky one's Jotunheim—the world of primal storms. And the other one has to be Muspelheim, the world of primal fire. Nothing lives there but killer giants."

"What's *that?*" Michael said, staring downward and to the left.

Audrey looked. "Hel," she said simply.

"I always thought hell would be hot," Summer said, her eyes widening like cornflowers blooming.

"Hel, with one *l*. It's the underworld, where everything sinks in the end. Ruled by Hella, queen of the dead."

It looked like a frozen lake, colder and blacker than the empty space between the worlds. Jenny had never seen such a lightless, joyless place.

The bridge to it was like a slide, broad and frosty.

"We *definitely* wouldn't want to go there. Or to that one—the one that looks like a cavern. That's Svartalfheim, the subterranean world."

"No more caves, thank you," Michael said.

There was only one island left. It was the one directly below them, and both ends of the bridge they stood on seemed connected to it. From here, the surface was obscured by dark mist and shadows.

Audrey said, "Niflheim, land of ice and shadows. The Shadow World." She shook her head. "I still don't believe this."

"Why not? It's no weirder than anything else we've seen today," Dee said. "But I only count eight worlds. Where's Earth?"

Audrey looked around, then shrugged. "Maybe we don't get to see that bridge until we finish the Game."

"Who cares? Look, we wanted to walk between the worlds, right?" Dee said, her eyes shining. "And now we're doing it. So—shall we?"

Jenny nodded. She felt very tiny and insignificant standing here, and her throat was tight. And she had the feeling that it was going to be harder going down than going up—because now the fall was so much longer.

They started moving. It was hard to walk in the place between the worlds—physically hard. After two or three steps Jenny began to feel muscle-burn in her calves and thigh muscles. She could hear Audrey panting in front of her.

And the barest glimpse of the fall on either side made Jenny's internal organs feel as if they were plunging out of her body.

Her legs wanted to freeze. She wanted to get down on her rump and scoot the rest of the way—no, get down on her stomach and *slither.* But that wasn't the worst.

She was afraid she would faint.

If I faint up here, I'll fall. Of course I'll fall. Nobody faints neatly forward. I'll slide off the side.

The moment the thought of fainting occurred to her, it blocked everything else out. She *was* going to faint. Just thinking about it made her dizzy. She was so scared of fainting, she felt like jumping.

Hysteria began to bubble up inside her. She shouldn't have thought about jumping. Now she was afraid she *would* jump, just because the idea had occurred to her. She had to try not to think about it.

Think of anything else. Think of Tom, think of getting to Tom. But the idea of jumping was now stuck in her mind. She started to picture it. She could get it all over with, turn to the side and just let go. God, no—she didn't want to, but she was afraid she'd go crazy and do it. . . .

The voice came from her own brain, but it was so harsh it seemed alien. *You keep on moving, girl!*

Jenny realized she was stopped, frozen. Staring

down at her own feet in their brown leather hiking boots, and the white ribbon of bridge, and the formless darkness on either side.

Just put one foot in front of the other. The right foot. Put out your right foot.

I can't, she thought.

Yes, you can!

But if I faint—or jump—

You expect everybody else to face their fears, and you can't face yours? You're not *your only master if you can't even control your own feet! You're just a coward!*

The right boot jerked a little and stepped forward.

That's right. Now the other one.

The other boot came forward. Jenny was walking again.

She could do it—command her own feet. Just put one foot in front of the other. And one more step. And one more.

Don't look to the side. One more step. And one more.

There were only a few body-lengths of bridge in front of her. She could see where it ended. Ten feet. Five feet.

On legs that had suddenly gone weak as angel-hair pasta, Jenny stumbled and fell onto safe ground.

Dee bent over her. "You okay?"

Weakly Jenny patted one of Dee's hightops. "I'm terrific, thanks."

"I shouldn't have let you be last. I forgot."

Jenny sat up and wiped her forehead. "I did fine by myself."

"Yeah, you did. You seem to be doing a lot of that these days."

Jenny was very happy.

Then it hit her. They were across. They'd made it.

Tom.

She looked up so fast her vision swam.

After the alien grandeur of the place between the worlds, it was something of a comedown. They were on the central island in the artificial lake at Joyland Park. The lighthouse looked the same as it had all night, white and shining. The park around them was a riot of lights—but ordinary lights, illuminating ordinary rides like the SuperLooper and the Tumblebug. Everything looked very ordinary.

Behind her, the bridge arched gracefully over the lake water, and the water reflected a wavering arch back. There was no mist, and no sign of any other worlds. The top of the arch wasn't more than forty feet high.

"A hallucination, I guess," Audrey said slowly. "One of Julian's things. And I suppose it must have been from me, since I'm the only one who knew about those other worlds."

Jenny opened her mouth, then shut it again. She thought Audrey must be right—but she wasn't sure. And the truth was that they would probably never be sure.

She looked back at the lighthouse. "Come on, people. This is it."

When she got up her legs were shaky, but she took the lead and Dee let her.

The lighthouse looked bigger as they got closer. It

was life-size, with a widow's walk around the top and a weathercock. And it was attached to some broad dark building that Jenny hadn't seen before because it wasn't lit up. A restaurant, maybe, she thought.

There was a wooden door in the lighthouse's side, with a large iron handle.

"Monster positions," Dee reminded Jenny as she reached for the handle. Then Dee stood ready to kick the door shut if anything unfriendly was behind it.

"Tom and Zach will be at the top, of course," Michael said, resting with his hands on his thighs in anticipation.

But they weren't.

It was funny, how the end began. Jenny had been waiting for so long, working and fighting, and all the time *waiting* for the moment that she would see Tom. She was so used to waiting she wasn't really ready for it to end. She wasn't—prepared.

She almost couldn't deal with it.

But when it started happening, it happened fast, and prepared or not, she was thrown into it.

She pulled on the iron handle, and the wooden door swung open. There was no need for Dee to kick it shut. Everything inside was illuminated, and nothing came rushing toward them.

Black metal stairs curved up on Jenny's left, circling upward toward the top of the lighthouse. But straight in front of her she could see the interior of the broad building. The lighthouse had no back wall, and opened right into it.

It was a wonderful place, with a huge diorama two stories high as a backdrop. It looked like a movie set of a wharf scene, but the numbered flags on poles betrayed its real purpose. It was an indoor miniature golf course.

"Treasure Island," Michael said, peering around her shoulder. "Pirates, see?"

It was pirates. The diorama featured a mural painted on the far wall of the broad building, a marvelously realistic mural with a volcano in the background. Painted smoke and little neon lights for sparks showed that it was erupting. There was also a mammoth storm in the painted sky, and forked lightning that really flashed.

At the bottom of the mural, just behind the golf course itself, two dinghies were landing on some fiberglass rocks. One boat was painted, with a pirate in an eye patch and hat, a lace cravat, and boots.

The other boat was real, with Tom and Zach.

Jenny touched her mouth. Then she was running.

There weren't any words for what she felt next. When she'd been separated from Tom in the paper house, it had been for hours. This time it had been days. She was exhausted, overstressed, starving, on the verge of collapse—and she'd never been so happy in her life.

Just the sight of him brought back everything that was good and homelike to her mind. It was like coming back to her own room after being away a long time with strangers.

It was where she belonged.

She threw her arms around him. And then she just held on, her heart pounding and pounding.

"Watch out, Jenny. He was here just a minute ago."

And Jenny, who had for so long associated Tom with protection, with safety and security and coziness, found herself feeling passionately protective of Tom. As if he were Summer. Looking into his dear face, handsome and rather brooding just now, and his wonderful green-flecked eyes, she said, "Don't worry. I'll take care of you."

"Just let me *out,* please," Tom said sharply, and then gave up and kissed her back. Jenny's solicitous feelings had thrown her into a perfect spasm of love for him, and it felt *so good* to kiss him again.

"If you two could tear yourself apart for just a minute . . ." Zach's voice said.

Jenny looked up. Her cousin was in the back of the dinghy, yes, the same cousin she'd lost, she thought a little deliriously. Exactly the same, with his wonderful beaky nose and his ash-blond hair pulled back in a casual ponytail and his keen gray eyes.

"I missed you, too," she said and scrambled back to hug him.

"We're tied up," Tom said briskly.

Jenny saw that his brown wrists were tied behind his back with some kind of thick cord. "No problem," she said, just as briskly, and pulled out the Swiss Army knife. I'll never go anywhere without one again, she thought, and, crouching by Zach's feet, she began carefully sawing at the cord.

"Hi, Dee," Tom said, calm as if he were meeting her Saturday at the ball game. "Hey, Audrey, Mi—" He broke off and bolted upright, and Jenny cut his hand.

"Sit *down,"* she said.

He didn't seem to notice. *"Summer?"*

"Hi, Tom," Summer said shyly.

"Summer?"

"She wasn't dead, just asleep," Audrey said.

Jenny said, "Sit *down,* will you? We'll explain later."

"Yeah—sure," Tom said weakly. He sat down. Jenny finished cutting the cord enough so that he could pull out of it. Then, while he was rubbing his hands, she turned to Zach.

"Are you both okay?" she added. "I mean—not hurt or anything?"

"We're fine," Tom said absently. "He just put us here a little while ago. We were in the lighthouse, before, and it wasn't too bad—except I was afraid you'd come."

"You *knew* I'd come. I hope."

"I hoped you wouldn't. I was afraid you would."

"Tom"—a strand on Zach's cord sprang apart—"you don't have to worry about me." She looked up to find him looking down at her, in that new way, the way he had since the end of Julian's first Game. As if she were something infinitely precious, something that bewildered him, but amazed him—something he didn't deserve, but trusted.

"Sure I have to worry about you, Thorny," he said simply. "Just like you worry about me."

Jenny smiled.

"Nobody needs to worry right now. We've won the Game, Tom. We went on the treasure hunt and now we've found you. It's all over."

"I'll still be happier out of here," he said, and Zach said, "That goes for me doubled, tripled, and quadrupled."

Jenny glanced around. She supposed it was a spooky place in a way—if you were sitting and anticipating trouble. There were real cave entrances below the mural, leading to other parts of the miniature golf range. There were mock buildings holding the same thing—golf holes—with names like Lafitte's Black Powder Works. It was dark inside all these places.

"Don't tell me. You guys were afraid of the parrot," Michael said. Jenny followed his gaze to a section of the building beside the golf course, apparently an area for eating, because there were orange plastic tables and stools bolted to the ground. There was also a small stage with a sign that read: CAP'N BILL AND SEBASTIAN, THE WONDER PARROT. Also a mounted TV showing Woody Woodpecker cartoons, mercifully silent.

"No, we were afraid of the eyes," Tom said, stepping out of the dinghy and over a length of thick rope that sagged between two wharf pillars.

Jenny's head snapped up. "The eyes?"

"The ones that sit in the shadows and look at you. And the whispering."

Jaw squared, Jenny sawed through the last of Zach's cord and rubbed his wrists. So the other Shadow Men were around.

Tom was staring at Audrey's arm. "What happened to *you?*"

"Believe me, you're happier not knowing."

"You guys all look like you've been playing with the Raiders—and losing," Tom said.

It was true, Jenny thought, following Zach over the rope. The prisoners they'd come to rescue looked fine, just as they had when they'd disappeared behind Julian's wall of fire. A little crumpled and stained about the clothes, but otherwise fine. Zach still had his 35 millimeter camera around his neck.

It was the rescuers who were bloody and battered. Even Summer looked wounded, like a broken-stemmed flower. Audrey, usually the picture of elegance, looked more like a young hiker who'd been in a bad accident. Dee's jeans were stained dark at the thigh. Michael looked as if he'd been ducked in swamp water and then tumble-dried.

"You've been through a lot," Zach said, and for once his gray eyes weren't cool or unreadable. "Thanks, Jenny."

Jenny waved dismissively, but she felt a glow inside. "What happened back there in the fire, anyway? One minute I was holding your hand, the next . . ."

"I fell," Zach said. "Pure dumb luck. I tripped, and when I got up, I didn't know which way to go. I stumbled around and ended up back in Julian's base."

"Out of the fire, into the frying pan," Michael said.

"And then Tom came back for me." Zach looked at Tom, and something passed between them without words. The introverted photographer and the star athlete had never been particularly close before, but Jenny had the feeling that that had changed now. She was pleased.

"Aww," Michael said.

Audrey said, "Shut up—*mon cher.*"

Dee interrupted. "Here's a map of the park." The

map was wood, painted to look like parchment, with iron chains around it.

"It *is* an amusement park, then. We could see some of it out the lighthouse window," Tom said. "Okay, look, here's my plan. . . ."

His voice trailed off. Audrey, Michael, Dee, and Summer weren't looking at him. Instead, they were looking at Jenny expectantly.

Tom looked at Zach, who was standing with his arms folded, something like amusement in his sharp-featured face.

"Okay, uh—why don't you tell us *your* plan?" Tom said to Jenny.

Jenny was fighting amusement, too. "I don't have one. We don't *need* one. We've won, and we ought to be able to just walk out of here. The only thing I don't understand is why Julian hasn't shown up."

They all looked at the various dark doorways and crevices.

"Do you think maybe—he's watching us?" Summer said.

"Of course I'm watching; that's what I do," a weary voice said.

14

Jenny spun. Julian was standing beside a ticket booth with a brass telescope on top. He was surrounded by ferns and fake palms. And he looked—tired?

He was wearing the duster jacket again, and he had his hands in his pockets. His hair was as white as a winter moon.

It was up to her to face him, Jenny knew. She was the only one who could do this.

She stepped forward. She tried to look him directly in the eyes, but it was hard. His gaze seemed curiously veiled—as if he wasn't exactly looking at her, but through her.

"We've won," she said with more confidence than she felt. "Finally. It's the last Game, and this time there's no way you can bend the rules. You have to let us go."

What *was* the look in those eyes? They were midnight-colored and full of shadows—but there was something else, something Jenny only recognized when she felt a presence beside her. Tom was there, looking devilishly handsome and full of cold, protective fury. He wasn't going to let her face Julian alone. His hand rested on her shoulder, lightly, not possessively. As if to say he was there to back her up, whatever happened.

"I ought to try to kill you," he said to Julian. "I can't, but I sure ought to try. I will, if you pull anything this time."

Julian ignored him completely.

Wistfulness, Jenny thought. That was it. Julian wasn't exactly looking at Tom, but for a moment he'd glanced at Tom's hand on her shoulder—and there was wistfulness in his eyes.

The Shadow Man seeing the one thing he could never have, she thought. Human love.

"Are you going to pull anything?" Tom asked tightly.

It was a good question. Jenny was braced for some kind of a trick, too—ready to fight Julian, to argue him out of it. Every other time they'd won a Game, Julian had unveiled some weird twist at the last minute, had found some way to crush them and laugh at them.

Jenny had fully expected him to try it again this time—so why hadn't he? Why hadn't he appeared before they got Tom and Zach untied? Why wasn't he dressed as a pirate, fending them off with a cutlass, smiling and pointing out that they had to *get* to Tom and Zach to rescue them? Why wasn't he playing the Game?

Probably because he has something worse up his

sleeve, she told herself. That painted volcano will erupt. Real lightning will strike. Or maybe—

—or maybe he was just tired of playing.

"We *have* won, haven't we?" she said, suddenly uncertain. She would have thought she would enjoy announcing her victory more than this.

"You've won," Julian said, and there was no emotion in his voice. He still wasn't really looking at her. And he did seem tired—his whole body looked tired.

He looked—defeated.

"So—I can leave."

"Yes."

Jenny was still looking for the catch. "And take everyone with me."

"Yes."

"Even Tom. I can take Tom with me."

"Let's go," Tom said abruptly, his fingers closing around her upper arm. Jenny almost—not quite—shook him off. This wasn't like Julian at all.

"I can go and I can take Tom," she persisted. "And everyone. It's the last Game, and it's over now."

For the first time Julian looked at her. His eyes were fully dilated, with the look Jenny had seen in the cave. An inward look, as if nothing mattered. It was too brittle to be bitter. A look like blue ice about to break up and fall into dark water.

A—shattering.

"It's the last Game," he said. "It's over now. I won't bother you again."

The corner of his mouth jerked as if he were about to say something more—or maybe it was involuntary. Then, without speaking, he whirled around.

"Get out. Get her out." Without looking at Tom, he spoke in a distorted voice, thick with restraint. "Get her out of here! Before I do—something—"

"Julian—" Jenny said.

"—we'll all be sorry for—"

He gave a shudder of suppressed emotion.

Tom grabbed Jenny's other arm and wheeled her in the opposite direction.

There was a rough wooden door standing on the far side of the building. It was set between two enormous stones, like a gate. But there was no fence or wall, just the door standing in space and looking tremendously solid, as if it had always been there.

It was partly open, and inside Jenny could see her grandfather's hallway, including the small telephone table with the white doily on it. The phone was lying on the floor where it had fallen, receiver off the hook.

"Home," Audrey said, in a voice of such startled longing that Jenny almost yielded to Tom's steering hands. But then she twisted away.

Insanely, inexplicably, she wanted to stay and talk to Julian.

Julian didn't want to talk to her.

"Leave. Just *go*—now!"

Even without seeing his face, she could tell that his control was breaking. She tried to turn him around.

"Jenny, are you *crazy?*" Dee said. Dee and Tom were both pulling at Jenny now, trying to get her away from Julian.

"Just give me one minute!"

"Will you get her *out* of here!" Julian snarled.

Everyone was shouting. Summer was crying. And Jenny was having to fight off the two people she loved best—Tom and Dee—for a reason she couldn't even explain clearly to herself.

She knew the risk; she understood why Summer was crying. She could feel the storm building in Julian. The air was hot and electric, as if heat lightning were about to explode. He could do *anything* to them.

But she couldn't let it go.

"Julian, please listen—"

He turned, then, whirling so fast that Jenny stepped back. She was frightened by what she saw in his face.

"You cannot save me from myself," he hissed, saying each word distinctly, biting it off. Then he looked Tom straight in the face. "Get her out of here. I am trying to play this Game by the rules. But if you don't have her out in thirty seconds, all bets are off."

"I'm sorry, Thorny," Tom said and picked her up.

"No!" Jenny was furious at the indignity, at being made to go where she didn't want to go, like a child. And she was furious because she had just discovered the reason that she wanted to stay. Julian had said it for her. She wanted to save him.

It was like the sign on Aba's mirror. *Do no harm. Help when you can. Return good for evil.* That was what she wanted, to help if she could. To return good for evil where it had the chance of making a difference.

But Tom wasn't the only one she'd have to fight. Dee was marching along beside him, eyes fixed grimly on Jenny. And Michael and Audrey, Zach and Summer were surrounding them, forming a tight little knot to escort Jenny home.

"We're gonna drag you through that door by your hair, if we have to, Sunshine," Dee said, just in case this wasn't sufficiently clear.

"There are times when you can be *too good,* and this is one of them," Audrey added.

They all started for the door—but they never got there.

The mist was different from the fog that had risen around Jenny on the bridge. It was thick, interspersed with dark tendrils, and it moved *fast.*

Ice and shadows. A whirling, seething mixture of white and black.

Jenny remembered it very well—she'd seen it twice before. Once when she was five years old, in a memory so terrible that she had repressed it completely, giving herself amnesia. And once a month ago, when she'd relived the memory in Julian's paper house.

Tom was turning, enraged, to shout at Julian. Jenny slid from his arms. She could see by Julian's face that he had nothing to do with this.

Looking around was like being plunged into a nightmare—a recurring nightmare. Frost was forming on every surface. It was creeping up the wooden poles with rusty lanterns that stood throughout the golf course. It was coating the barrels labeled XXX and the boxes labeled BLACK POWDER. Icicles were growing on the tarred ropes linking the wharf pillars.

Freezing wind blew Jenny's hair straight back from her face, then whipped it stingingly across her cheeks.

"What's happening?" Audrey screamed. "What's happening?" Summer was just screaming.

It was so *cold*—as cold as the water that had drowned her in the mine shaft. So cold that it hurt. It hurt to breathe and it hurt to stand still.

Tom was shouting in her ear, trying to lift her and stagger toward the door. He'd made it through the fire. . . .

But not now. The ice storm was blinding. The white light was painfully brilliant, and the dark tendrils lashed through it like whips, like supple reaching arms.

They were holding Tom still. They were trapping everyone.

Slowly the wind died down. The blinding brightness faded. Jenny could see again, and she saw that the dark mist was gathering itself, coalescing. Forming figures.

Figures with malevolent, ancient eyes.

The other Shadow Men had come.

"Oh, God," Audrey whispered. She drew in closer to Jenny. There were ice crystals in her spiky copper bangs. "Oh, God—I didn't *know*. . . ."

Jenny hadn't known, either. She didn't understand. She recognized the cruel and ravenous eyes—she couldn't be wrong about them. But the forms that went with the eyes . . .

Michael wiped his mouth with the back of his hand, placing himself in front of Audrey. Summer was making small clotted sounds of fear. Zach's eyes glazed, then he shook his head and pulled Summer nearer to the group.

Those—things—can't be Shadow Men, Jenny thought. The Shadow Men are beautiful. Heartbreakingly beautiful.

These creatures were terrible.

They were hideously twisted and deformed. It would have been easier if they hadn't looked at all like humans, but they did. They were like dreadful, obscene parodies of human people.

Some of them had skin like leather—real leather, like something that had been smoked and cured. Yellowish-brown, so hard that their faces could never change expression. Others had skin like toadstool flesh—corpse-white and frilled, with dangling wattles.

It wasn't just the skin. Their bodies were distorted and maimed, and their faces were terrible. One had no nose, just an empty black hole. Another had no facial orifices of any kind. Nothing—only blank, stretched skin where eyes and nose and mouth should be. Another had a horn growing out of the back of its head.

And the *smell*—they smelled like decay, and like brimstone. Jenny's nostrils stung, and she felt bile rise in her throat.

Beside her, Tom was breathing hard. She looked at him, saw the open horror in his green-flecked eyes. Dee's nostrils were flared, and she was holding herself ready for an attack.

It came suddenly—one of the creatures scuttling across the tiled floor, to stop right in front of Jenny. Jenny gasped—and recognized it. It was the gray and withered fetus they'd seen in the park, the one that had scampered into the Whip. Now that she saw it more closely, it didn't look young like a fetus at all. It looked old, impossibly old, so old that it had shrunk and caved in on itself.

"Oh, God . . ." Audrey whispered again. Summer was keening.

Dee had fallen into the Cat stance, perfectly balanced, ready to initiate any action.

"Should I do it?" she said through clenched teeth.

Jenny opened her mouth, but before she could say anything, the withered fetus spoke.

"Can we take you? We can carry you," it said, looking at Jenny with eyes that glowed like a tiger's.

Then it giggled, wildly and obscenely, and scuttled away.

I never asked Julian what the little creatures were, Jenny remembered. She had been certain they weren't Shadow Men because they were so hideous. Now she looked toward him, hoping that he would have some explanation, that he would tell her what she was thinking was wrong.

He had stepped forward. There was a dusting of ice on his black jacket, and his hair glimmered as if it were made from frost. His beautifully sculpted face and mouth had never looked more perfect.

"What are they?" Jenny whispered.

"My ancestors," he said, introducing them to her, and destroying her last hope.

"Those—things?" She still couldn't connect them to Julian.

Without any emotion that she could discern he said, "That's what we become. That's what I'll become. It's inevitable."

Jenny shook her head.

"How?" Zach said sharply. He was probably the least repulsed, Jenny thought vaguely—that photog-

rapher's mind of his. He found grotesque things interesting.

But Jenny didn't. Not things like this, oh, never things like this.

"Is that—what they *really* look like? Or is it to scare us?" she heard her own voice saying.

Julian's strangely veiled gaze met hers. "Those are their true forms." He looked them over expressionlessly. "We're born in perfection," he said, without either modesty or arrogance—without *any* feeling that Jenny could see. "But as we age, we become grotesque. It's inevitable—the outer form changes to reflect our inner nature." He shrugged. "We become monsters."

The poem. The poem on her grandfather's desk, Jenny thought. She understood it at last, the line about them fingering old bones. These were the kind of creatures who would sit in a pit and do that. From Julian's beauty she would never have guessed, could never have pictured him that way.

Now she tried to keep it out of her mind, the picture of Julian looking like *them,* so distorted, so debased. It *couldn't* happen to him—but he'd said it was inevitable.

"But I don't know what they're doing here now," Julian continued, as if unaware of her reaction. "This isn't their Game; they have nothing to do with it."

"You're wrong," a tall Shadow Man said. It had the eyes of a crocodile. Its voice, though, was shockingly beautiful, distant and lonely as wind chimes of ice.

"It became our Game when she stole our prey," said another one, this one in the voice of somebody who'd eaten ground glass and fishhooks.

"Who stole your prey?" Tom shouted. But Jenny felt as if the floor had suddenly dropped away beneath her.

Her little fingers and the sides of her hands were prickling as if small shocks were going through them. She looked at Julian.

Julian had frozen, hands in pockets, staring hard at the other Shadow Men. Then his eyebrows lifted minutely and his head tilted back slightly. He'd got it.

His eyes, still expressionless, shifted to Jenny.

"She took the old man," a third Shadow Man explained, in a whispering voice like snow blowing. "And the two boys, those were our prey, too. We hunted them. They belonged to us."

Suddenly voices joined in from all around Jenny.

"The old man was ours by right," a voice like a brass gong said.

"Blood right," a thick and muddy voice croaked.

"He made the bargain—his life was ours," a voice like a cat-o'-nine-tails added.

Julian looked the way Audrey's mother had once, when she had suggested Michael give his filthy sneakers to Goodwill. "But you were done with the old man—surely," he said fastidiously.

"We hadn't finished enjoying him."

"He was ours—forever."

"And the boys," a voice like cold wind put in, "we'd just started with the boys."

"Never got a tooth in them. . . ."

I'm glad, Jenny thought fiercely. She was glad she'd saved her grandfather, too, saved him from an eternity with these monsters. But she was still frightened.

The tall Shadow Man was moving forward. It looked down at Jenny with its crocodile eyes: ancient, pitiless, and endlessly malevolent.

"She stole their souls from us," it said formally, making the claim. "And now her life is forfeit. She is our rightful prey."

There was a burst of noise, rising and swelling from every corner of the room. It got louder and louder. It was composed of beautiful sounds and strident ones intermixed, wailing and yelping and pure tones like music.

The Shadow Men were laughing.

"Get out of here, you crazy bastards! Go away!" Dee shouted over the cacophony. She ran toward the assembled monsters, punching straight out from the shoulder, snapping her arm forward to hit with a flattened hand. She kicked, her legs flashing out too fast for the eye to follow, striking with devastating force.

"No!" Jenny screamed, plunging after her. "Dee!"

She did it without thinking, and Tom was beside her, ready to stop Dee or help her fight, depending on what the Shadow Men did.

Jenny was afraid they'd *kill* Dee. Julian had been able to throw Dee across the room without effort. But the Shadow Men just laughed more and more uproariously—and faded wherever Dee kicked.

Dee's hands and feet never struck anything solid; the monsters melted like shadows whenever she touched them.

She was panting and exhausted when Jenny and Tom reached her.

The action had cleared Jenny's head. She glanced at Julian, who was still standing where he had been, apparently unaffected by the sight of Dee going crazy. He looked—remote. Not tired, as he had before, but—disconnected. As if this were all a moderately interesting play. Maybe he was sympathizing with the other Shadow Men.

Jenny looked at the one with the crocodile eyes. She nerved herself to speak to it.

"You're saying that because I released my grandfather's soul, you have some right to me."

"By law, you're now ours," the tall Shadow Man said. "We can take you—embrace you—do what we like with you." Unexpectedly it looked at Julian. "The law can't be changed."

"I know the law can't be changed," Julian said flatly.

"She cheated us ten years ago—kept us from tasting her flesh—but now she belongs to us," the chilling, musical voice said.

And then, as quickly as that, it was happening. The dark mist was closing around Jenny, separating her from Tom and Dee. She heard Tom cry out. The mist was like cold hands touching her body. The freezing wind was howling in her ears. She was being dragged away, just as they had dragged her grandfather into the closet years ago.

15

What came next was not a verbal shout—if it had been, Jenny would have thought it was Tom. It wasn't even a word exactly, more a wave of energy. And the energy was sheer negation, opposition. *No! No!*

Stop.

The mist uncoiled. Jenny's vision unblurred. She was standing, gasping, a little closer to one of the cave entrances. Tom and Dee were shaking their heads, wiping their faces, as if to get rid of some blinding haze. They were panting, too. Everyone seemed on the verge of hysteria. But the shout had come from Julian.

He was standing in the middle of the room. Desperate hope leaped inside Jenny—maybe there was something he could do. But the next moment the hope folded and collapsed.

"You know the law," the tall Shadow Man repeated blandly.

And Julian's eyes fell.

They're playing with us, Jenny realized dimly. With Julian, too; they like to see anybody suffer. They didn't stop because he yelled at them, they stopped so they could draw it out a little longer.

Another Shadow Man spoke. This one had liver-colored skin, with splotches here and there as if he'd been burned by acid. The white of one of his eyes wasn't white at all, it was red, red as rubies, red as blood.

"Nothing can stop us from taking her—unless someone else is willing to go in her place."

It took Jenny several heartbeats to get her mind around that. She wasn't thinking properly anymore. Then she remembered—her grandfather. They'd said exactly the same thing to him. *A life for a life. Someone must go in her place.* And her grandfather had, and now Jenny had rescued him and broken the bargain, and brought everything back to the starting place.

And meanwhile the terrible silence went on and on and on.

Then she heard a voice, a voice that was quite calm and devil-may-care—and human.

"I'll go."

Tom had stepped forward. His dark brown hair was neat and short and his smile was rakish. He said it as if he were offering to go out and get pizza for the baseball team.

And he looked *wonderful.* Somehow he managed to make his rumpled and frost-touched clothes look like the latest fashion. He stood casually, and there wasn't a trace of fear in his expression.

For a moment, without thinking of anything else, Jenny was simply proud of him. Fiercely, *passionately* proud that a human, a seventeen-year-old who hadn't even heard of the Shadow Men until a month ago, could stand up to them like this. Could conceal his terror and smile that way and offer to die.

That's how I want to die, Jenny thought, and a strange serenity came over her. I want to do it *well*—since it has to be done. And I hope I have the courage, and I think—I really do think—that I just might. We'll see.

Because of course there was no possibility of letting them take Tom. She would never allow that.

Before she could say so, though, there was a short, wild laugh. Dee was beside Tom, her head thrown back, her eyes flashing like a jaguar's. She was as beautiful as some goddess of the night—some *warrior* goddess who'd just sprung up to defend her people. And she was grinning, the old barbaric grin that contrasted so oddly with her delicate features. The grin that Jenny hadn't seen since Audrey had gotten hurt.

"No," she said to Tom. "*You* won't go. I will." She was breathing very quickly, and laughing—she seemed almost exuberant. "Jenny needs you, you jerk. She'd never let you do it. *I'll* go."

"Just back off, Dee," Tom said softly. His eyes were oddly tranquil, even dreamy, but there was something frightening in his voice. At any other time, Jenny thought, Dee would have backed off.

Now she just laughed. She looked like Dee—reckless, warlike, and unconditionally loyal—but she looked like *more* than herself, too. A greater Dee.

"It's my choice," she said. "I know what I'm getting into."

And then, as Jenny listened in disbelief, other voices joined in.

"She's my cousin," Zach said. His face was sharp as a blade, and there was an intense, clear light in his gray eyes. He moved to stand sword-straight beside Dee. "I'm her blood relative. If anyone goes, it should be me."

Audrey and Michael had been whispering hastily together; now they stepped forward. Audrey's burnished copper hair was loose on her shoulders, and with her white clothing she looked like some kind of virgin sacrifice. Not elegant but exquisite, and holding herself with pride. Her skin was camellia-pale, and her voice was cool and steady.

"If everybody else is going to be a hero, then we can, too," she said. "The truth is that Jenny's worth more than any of us, and we all know it. So, now. You can take your pick." She looked at the Shadow Men. She very nearly, Jenny thought, tossed her head.

"Yeah," Michael said. "The only thing is, we figure we'll go together, her and me. You know, for company, right?" He gave a No Big Deal shrug, and then his mouth trembled violently, and he grabbed for Audrey's hand. He looked for a moment as if he were going to be sick, but then he wiped his mouth and stood facing the Shadow Men squarely. There was a curious dignity about his stocky little figure.

Jenny's throat was so swollen that she could barely breathe. She was opening her mouth, though, when something like a small blue thunderbolt shot into the clear space in the middle of the room.

"Oh, please don't take Jenny," Summer gasped. She was looking utterly terrified and as fragile as spun glass, and there was a wild blankness in her eyes. Her words came in an incoherent rush. "Please—please—you *can't* take her. I'm not brave or smart—I should have been dead in the paper house. I—"

That was as far as she got. She collapsed like a bird shot out of the sky, and lay in a pool of blue until Zach picked her up. He held her—Zach, who never paid attention to any girl.

The Shadow Men were pleased. Jenny could tell. This was probably turning out to be a much better game than they ever could have hoped—much better *sport.* They had seven mice to play with, and they were clearly loving it.

"Are you sure you know what you're offering?" the one with the crocodile eyes asked gravely.

"We could explain to them," the one with the bloodred eye suggested.

"Tell them exactly what they're in for."

"How we mean to enjoy them." Other voices joined in, and the Shadow Men moved in closer. A wave of revulsion went through Jenny at the sight of them, as if she were seeing them for the first time. They were old as spiders, old as stone. They were—abominations. And the thought of them touching any of her friends was insufferable.

It was time somebody put a stop to this.

"That's enough," she said in a voice as sharp and dictatorial as Audrey's. "You've had your fun, but the game's over. I'm the one you want, the one that cheated you. So forget everybody else. Let's go."

That was *good,* she thought, and a little wave of serenity came back. She was glad she could be as brave as the others. She was going to do this well, and that was all that counted now.

The Shadow Men seemed to know it was over, too. The red-eyed one held out a hand to her almost gently. It had fingers like a gorilla's—black, padded, thick as sausages and coming to a point at the ends.

Jenny put her hand in his.

The Shadow Man lifted his lips to show long, blunt teeth like tusks.

Something knocked them apart.

Jenny was knocked breathless, too, startled and confused. She thought it was some sort of attack.

It was Julian.

His hair was shining like lightning, like quicksilver. His whole being seemed full of elemental energy—of frightening intensity. And his eyes were the unbelievable, luminous blue of the precise moment before dawn.

He looked at Jenny for just one second, and then he turned and she could only see the clean purity of his profile.

"Go through the door!" he said. "That's your way home. They won't come after you."

He was between her and the Shadow Men. And apparently, unlike Dee, he could interact with them physically. At any rate, they were keeping back.

"Go on!" he shouted.

"We must have blood," the crocodile-eyed Shadow Man said. "We *will* have blood."

"Hurry!" Julian shouted.

Through the open door Jenny could see her grandfather's hallway.

"We have a right to a kill," the crocodile-eyed Shadow Man said. From the air he snatched up something long and flat and incredibly ancient-looking. His fingers were covered in scaly skin like a dinosaur's, Jenny saw. Then she realized what the long, flat branch must be.

A runestave. Like the picture in her grandfather's journal, except that this one was real—was *more* real than any object Jenny had ever seen. It was like some of the island worlds—the ones that were brighter and more substantial-looking than Earth. This stave was so real that it looked *alive,* throbbing with raw power.

There were not just single runes carved on it, but lines and lines of them, tall and needle-thin. Even though they were delicately inscribed, each stroke stood out clearly. It was as if the cuts were filled with liquid diamond that shone against the background of wood.

Jenny couldn't keep looking at the runes. It was like trying to read in a dream—first the details were sharp, and then the whole stave seemed to be swarming with changes. The runes seemed to move before she could identify them.

That's the stave of life. If anything ever was, that's the stave of life, she thought.

The voice like faraway ice bells said, "Give her to us."

"No," Julian said.

Jenny felt movement behind her. Tom. And Dee,

and Zach supporting Summer, and Audrey and Michael together. They were all gathering near her, and their way was clear to the door. But nobody started for it.

"What's happening?" Audrey whispered.

"You know what we can do," the tall Shadow Man with the crocodile eyes said to Julian, and he held the runestave higher.

"Go through the door," Julian said, without turning.

"We can unmake you!" the tall one shrieked, and in that moment his voice wasn't beautiful. It was like an ice floe breaking, a cracking, smashing sound of destruction.

"What are they talking about?" Tom said.

His quiet, level voice helped Jenny. "They can cut out his name. If they cut out his name, he dies." Then she said, "Julian—"

"Go on!" he said.

The Shadow Men were very, very angry.

"We have a right to a kill!"

"Then take it!" Julian shouted. "But you won't get past me!"

The thin, scaly fingers of the Shadow Man's other hand were holding a knife. It looked like bone. It glittered like frost.

"Come on, Jenny," Tom said, not moving.

"Julian—"

"Go on!" Julian said.

The knife rose and fell.

Jenny heard herself scream. She saw the slash of the blade, the way the liquid diamond spilled like blood. There was a terrible gash in the stave now, a hideous blank space. A wound. They had carved out Julian's name.

Julian staggered.

Jenny wrenched herself away from something that was trying to hold her and fell on her knees beside him. Her thoughts were wheeling and spinning, with no order to them. There must be something to do, some way to help. . . .

Really, she knew by his face that it was too late.

The other Shadow Men were coming in a rush of darkness and freezing wind. Jenny looked up into the maelstrom and tried to lift Julian to his feet.

Then hands pulled at her. Human hands, helping her get Julian up. And then Jenny was running, they were all running, half carrying Julian with them, and the door was right in front of them.

Ice lashed at Jenny's back. A freezing tendril grabbed her ankle. But Michael was pushing the door open and Summer and Zach were falling through it—and then Audrey was through, and then she and Tom and Dee were, with Julian. She felt the resistance as she crossed the threshold, the g-force that threw her off balance and made her stumble and land on her knees.

The hallway was too small. There wasn't room for all of them, especially with Julian a dead weight. The telephone table went crashing sideways. People were falling on one another. Jenny was kneeling on somebody's leg.

"Get out of the way! We need to close the door!" Dee was shouting.

Everything was confusion. The leg under Jenny moved and she saw Audrey crawling away. She tried to crawl, too, dragging Julian. Tom picked up the telephone table and threw it over her head toward the living room.

Dee kicked the door shut just as the storm reached it.

"What about the circle?" Michael screamed. "Where's a knife? Where's a knife?"

Jenny knew she had a knife, but she couldn't move fast enough. Michael grabbed up something from the floor. It was a felt pen, the pen Jenny had used to sketch the rune circle. With a slashing motion, he crossed the circle out. The cross looked like a slanting *X,* like the rune Nauthiz. The rune of restraint.

"You don't need to do that," Julian said, and his voice was very distant. Powerless. "They won't come after you. They don't have a claim anymore."

He was lying on his back, eyes looking at the ceiling. He was holding his chest, as if the Shadow Men had cut out his heart instead of his name.

Jenny took his cold hands in hers.

So cold. As if he were a figure carved out of ice. His face was that pale, too, and his beauty was like a distant fire reflected in an icicle.

And it was strange, but at that moment Jenny seemed to see in him all the different ways he had looked before. All his many guises.

The boy in the More Games shop playing acid house music too loud. The Erlking, in white leather tunic and breeches. The Cyber-Hunter, in sleek body armor, with a blue triangle tattooed on his cheek. The masked dancer at the prom, in a black tuxedo and shirt.

It was as if each were a facet of a crystal reflecting back at her—and only now could she see the entire crystal for what it was.

Julian stepping out of the shadows, soft as a shadow himself. Julian wearing Zach's clothing, threatening her with the bees. Julian slipping the gold ring on her finger, sealing the bargain with a kiss. Julian leaning over her as she slept. Julian in the mining cave, his eyes dilated, his gaze shattering.

And she had never really found the right description for the color of those eyes. At times it had seemed close to this color or that color, but when you got down to it, words really failed. It wasn't like anything except itself.

Right now she thought she could see something flickering far back in his eyes, like a twisting blue flame in their depths.

"You can't die," she said, and she was surprised by how calm and matter-of-fact her voice was.

And Julian, although his eyes were looking somewhere past her, and his voice was weak, was equally calm. He almost seemed to be smiling.

"The law can't be changed," he said.

"You can't *die,"* Jenny said. Her fingers were very tight on his, but they only seemed to be getting colder.

Everyone else had moved away. Jenny wanted to tell them that they didn't need to, that everything was going to be all right. But somehow she knew better.

"Did you know that Gebo isn't just the rune of sacrifice?" Julian said.

"I don't care."

"It means a gift, too. You gave me a gift, you know."

"I don't care," Jenny said and began to cry.

"You showed me what it was like to love. What the universe could be like, *if."*

Jenny put her free hand to her mouth. She was sobbing without a sound.

"This is my gift to you now, and you can't help but take it. You're free, Jenny. They won't come after you again."

"You can't die," Jenny whispered raggedly around the tears. "There must be something to do. You can't just *go out—"*

Julian was smiling.

"No, I'll dream another dream," he said. "I've made up so many things, now I'll just go into one. I'll be part of it."

"All right," Jenny whispered. She suddenly knew that there was nothing to be done, nothing except to help him all she could. There was something in his face that told her—a peace that was already gathering. She wouldn't disturb that peace now. "You go into the dream, Julian."

"You don't blame me?"

"I don't blame you for anything."

"Whatever else I did, I loved you," he said. He stirred, and then added, "Maybe you'll dream about me sometime, and that will help get me there."

"I will. I'll dream you into a place without any shadows, only light."

He looked at her then, and she could see he wasn't afraid.

"Nothing really dies as long as it's not forgotten," he said.

And then blue mist seemed to gather in his eyes and obscure the flame.

"Go to the dream," Jenny whispered. "Go quick, now."

His chest was still, and she didn't think he heard her. But she caught the faintest breath of sound—not with her ears, but with her mind.

"Your ring . . ."

The hand that had been on his chest slipped, and Jenny saw the gold ring there. Jenny picked it up.

The inscription on the inside had changed. The words were no longer a spell to bind Jenny.

Before, it had said: *All I refuse & thee I chuse.*

Now it said simply: *I am my only master.*

16

The elemental energy, the quicksilver brightness, was gone from Julian's figure. Jenny was still holding his hand, but it suddenly seemed less substantial. She held tighter—and her fingers met.

Julian's body was dissolving into mist and shadows. In a moment even those had disappeared.

Just like that. Like smoke up a chimney.

Jenny sat back on her heels.

Then, slowly at first, but more quickly with each step, her friends gathered around her. Jenny felt Tom's arms, and felt that he was shaking.

She buried her head in his shoulder and held him as he held her.

It was Audrey and Michael who were the most helpful in what had to be done next. There were a lot of practical things to be handled.

Here in Pennsylvania the sun was just rising, and

home in California it was 3:00 in the morning. Audrey and Michael went next door and woke the neighbors up and asked if they could use a phone.

Then Audrey called her parents and woke *them* up, and asked if they could please wire some money. And Michael called his father and woke *him* up, and asked him to explain to everybody else's parents that all the kids were safe.

That was something for Jenny to hang on to, once Audrey and Michael had reported back. The thought that Michael's father would be calling Mr. and Mrs. Parker-Pearson and telling them Summer was coming home. Michael's father was a writer and slightly odd, but an adult, and therefore somewhat credible. Maybe they would even believe him.

Jenny really couldn't wait to see Summer's little brother's face.

And she wanted to see her parents, too, and her own little brother.

There were other things. Angela, P.C.'s almost-girlfriend, who would have to be told that P.C. was really and truly dead. And there would be the police to deal with again, and impossible questions to answer.

But she couldn't think about all that now. She was still thinking about Julian.

Nothing died if it wasn't forgotten—and she would never forget him. There would always be some part of him in her mind. Because of him, all her life she'd be more sensitive to the beauty of the world. To its—sensuality and immediacy. Julian had been a very *immediate* person.

The most extraordinary person she would ever meet, Jenny thought. Whimsical, quixotic, wild—*impossible.*

He had been so many things. Seductive as silver and deadly as a cobra. And vulnerable like a hurt child underneath it all.

Like a hurt child who could strike out with lethal accuracy, Jenny thought as she watched Audrey moving slowly around the living room, tidying things. He'd hurt Audrey badly, and if he hadn't quite killed Summer, it had been close. He'd let his Shadow Animals kill Gordie Wilson, who'd only been guilty of skipping school and killing rabbits.

The truth was that Julian had probably been too dangerous to live. The universe would be a much safer place without him.

But poorer. And more boring, definitely more boring.

It was Summer who said the astonishing thing.

"You know," she said, after twisting around on the living room couch to see if the cab was coming, "Julian said the world was evil and horrible—remember? But then he proved himself that it wasn't."

Jenny came out of her own thoughts and looked at Summer, amazed. That was it, exactly, of course. And that was why she could go on living, and even look forward to things. In a universe where *that* could happen, you *had* to go on living and hoping and doing your best. In a universe where that could happen, anything was possible.

That was Julian's real gift, she thought.

But there was another one, too, and she saw it as

she looked at the others. They had all changed—Julian had changed them. Like the rune Dagaz, the catalyst, he'd transformed everyone who met him.

Audrey and Michael—look at them. They were walking around holding hands. Audrey hadn't even bothered to put her hair up. Michael was patting her shoulder protectively.

And Dee and Audrey had been enemies a month ago. After tonight, Jenny didn't think they could ever be that way again.

Zach, now—Zach was looking at Summer with puzzled interest in his keen gray eyes. Like a scientist who finds himself unexpectedly fascinated by a new form of flower.

Won't last a week, Jenny thought. But it was good for Zach to notice girls, just the same. To have a human interest, something besides his own imagination and his photographs.

Julian had taught Zach that imagination wasn't always better than reality.

Summer is different, too, Jenny thought. She's not half as muddled as she used to be. That's why Zach's staring.

Now, Dee . . .

Jenny turned to look at her friend.

Dee was sitting instead of pacing, with one long leg stretched in front of her. She was looking very thoughtful, her head bent, her thickly lashed eyes narrowed.

Well, Dee was Dee, and would never change, Jenny thought lovingly.

But she was wrong. As she watched, Dee looked up at her and smiled.

"You know, I've been thinking. And I was thinking—it would mean a major change of plans, you see. It would mean a lot of studying, and I hate studying."

She stopped, and Jenny blinked, then leaned forward.

"Dee?"

"I'm thinking of maybe going to college after all. Maybe. I'm just barely entertaining the idea."

Dee had changed, too.

"Aba would be happy," Jenny said, and then she dropped it, because she was afraid that Dee would turn balky. Dee really hated being pushed.

"It's your own choice," was all she added.

"Yes, it is. Everything really is, isn't it? Our own choice."

Jenny looked down at the gold ring on her finger, then clasped her other hand over it. "A lot is."

And Tom was different—the fact that Jenny was wearing that ring showed how different. He hadn't said a word about it; she didn't even think he minded.

He *understood.*

If he hadn't, Jenny could never have been happy. As it was, she knew he wouldn't hate her if she tried to dream Julian into a wonderful dream. He might not want to hear about it, but he wouldn't be upset.

He didn't take her for granted anymore, and he didn't need to be possessive, either. Jenny thought that maybe he had changed the most of all.

Or maybe she had.

"The cab's here," Michael said. "Okay, so first we

have to go to the doctor. . . ." He stared at a scribbled list.

"No, first we go to the Western Union office, *then* the doctor," Audrey said, taking the list from him. "Then—"

"Then we *eat,*" Michael said.

"Après vous," Dee said, gesturing them through the door. When Audrey hiked a copper eyebrow at her, she grinned. "I can throw those fancy words around, too. *Bonjour. O solo mìo. Gesundheit."*

"D'accord," Audrey said and grinned back at her.

Zach and Summer went out. Jenny stopped for just an instant on the threshold, long enough to look back.

The hallway was empty, the door to the basement was shut. That was good. If any adults would listen to Jenny, she would have them make sure that door was never opened again.

She turned and went outside.

As they headed for the cab, Michael said the kind of thing that only Michael could say. The kind of thing that came from having a science fiction author as a dad.

"Look. What if—someday—somebody carved Julian's name *back* onto that runestave?" he said.

Tom stopped dead on the lush green grass for a moment. Then he started walking again, as Jenny put an arm through his. "Don't even talk about it," he said. "It'll never happen."

"No, I guess not. Just as well."

And Jenny, her arm entwined with Tom's, agreed—but, deep inside, some tiny part of her wondered.

She couldn't give in to the twinge of wistful sorrow she felt—she had a life to build. Things to consider. She couldn't just follow Tom to college now. She had to find out what she wanted to *do* with herself.

What do I like? she thought. Swimming. Computers. Cats. Helping people. Kids. Flowers.

She didn't know how she was going to put all those together—she'd have to find a way. After all, she was Jenny Thornton, her only master.

But just before she got into the cab, she looked up at the Pennsylvania sky. It was so blue—a bluer blue than California skies ever were in the morning. A beautiful, luminous color that seemed filled with promise.

If, someday, Julian should be reborn, she wished him well.

About the Author

LISA JANE SMITH realized she wanted to be a writer sometime between kindergarten and first grade. She got the idea for her first published book while baby-sitting in high school, and wrote it while attending college at the University of California at Santa Barbara (in between classes, of course).

Dreams and nightmares have always fascinated her. Many of her books, including *The Forbidden Game* trilogy, are based on her own nightmares and those of her friends. At times she stops in the middle of a particularly frightening dream and thinks, "This is awful. I sure hope I remember it when I wake up!"

She lives in a rambling house in the Bay Area of northern California with one dog, three cats, and about ten thousand books.

Now available from

Point Horror

T-shirts to make you *tremble!*

Want to be the coolest kid in the school? Then mosey on down to your local bookshop and pick up your Point Horror T-shirt and book pack.

Wear if you dare!

T-shirt and book pack available from your local bookshop now.

Point Horror Fans Beware!

Available now from Point Horror are tales for the midnight hour . . .

THE Point Horror TAPES

Two Point Horror stories are terrifyingly brought to life in a chilling dramatisation featuring actors from The Story Circle and with spine tingling sound effects.

Point Horror as you've never heard it before . . .

HALLOWEEN NIGHT
TRICK OR TREAT
THE CEMETERY
DREAM DATE

available now on audiotape at your nearest bookshop.

Listen if you dare . . .

Point Horror

Are you hooked on horror? Are you thrilled by fear? Then these are the books for you. A powerful series of horror fiction designed to keep you quaking in your shoes.

Titles available now:

The Cemetery
D.E. Athkins

The Dead Game
Mother's Helper
A. Bates

The Cheerleader
The Return of the Vampire
The Vampire's Promise
Freeze Tag
The Perfume
The Stranger
Twins
Caroline B. Cooney

April Fools
The Lifeguard
The Mall
Teacher's Pet
Trick or Treat
Richie Tankersley Cusick

Camp Fear
My Secret Admirer
Silent Witness
The Window
Carol Ellis

The Accident
The Invitation
The Fever
Funhouse
The Train
Nightmare Hall:
The Silent Scream
Deadly Attraction
The Roommate
The Wish
Guilty
The Scream Team
Diane Hoh

The Yearbook
Peter Lerangis

The Watcher
Lael Littke

The Forbidden Game:
The Hunter
The Chase
L.J. Smith

Dream Date
The Diary
The Waitress
Sinclair Smith

The Phantom
Barbara Steiner

The Baby-sitter
The Baby-sitter II
The Baby-sitter III
Beach House
Beach Party
The Boyfriend
Call Waiting
The Dead Girlfriend
The Girlfriend
Halloween Night
The Hitchhiker
Hit and Run
The Snowman
The Witness
R.L. Stine

Thirteen Tales of Horror
Various
Thirteen More Tales of Horror
Various
Thirteen Again
Various

Look out for:

Fatal Secrets
Richie Tankersley Cusick

Driver's Dead
Peter Lerangis

The Boy Next Door
Sinclair Smith

A terrifying series from Point Horror!

NIGHTMARE HALL

Where college is a

scream . . .

High on a hill overlooking Salem University, hidden in shadows and shrouded in mystery, sits Nightingale Hall.

Nightmare Hall, the students call it.

Because that's where the terror began . . .

Don't miss the spine-tingling thrillers in the Nightmare Hall series –

The Silent Scream
The Roommate
Deadly Attraction
The Wish
Guilty

POINT CRiME

If you like Point Horror, you'll love Point Crime!

A murder has been committed . . . Whodunnit?
Was it the teacher, the schoolgirl, or the best friend? An exciting series of crime novels, with tortuous plots and lots of suspects, designed to keep the reader guessing till the very last page.

Kiss of Death
School for Death
Peter Beere

Avenging Angel
Break Point
Final Cut
Shoot the Teacher
The Beat:
Missing Person
David Belbin

Baa Baa Dead Sheep
Jill Bennett

A Dramatic Death
Margaret Bingley

Driven to Death
Anne Cassidy

Overkill
Alane Ferguson

Death Penalty
Dennis Hamley

Concrete Evidence
The Smoking Gun
Malcolm Rose

Look out for:

Patsy Kelly Investigates:
A Family Affair
Anne Cassidy

The Beat:
Black and Blue
David Belbin

Deadly Music
Dennis Hamley